Sharp Edge

Tara Sharp Book Four

by *deadlines*

www.twelfthplanetpress.com

First published by Deadlines, October 2017
Copyright © 2017 by Marianne Delacourt
Editing by Alisa Krasnostein and Katharine Stubbs.
Copyediting by Elizabeth Disney.
Cover and text by Cathy Larsen Design

A catalogue record for this
book is available from the
National Library of Australia

To my clan: Helen Smith (the real Smitty), Debbie Phillips, Jo Pierce, Pam Haling, Michelle Fischer, Kath Holliday, Linda Curtin, Isobelle Carmody, Kaylen Jorgensen, Tania Heyblom, Ju Landéesse, Tracy Wilson, Joelene Pynnonen, Gabrielle Rogers, Amber Gwynne, Rachel Loffler, Robyn Smith and Nicola Scott.

Thank you for your love through the darkest of dark nights.

Sharp Edge

Marianne Delacourt

deadlines✳

Chapter 1

You are what you've been. I heard or read that somewhere.

It popped into my head as I lay on my bed, contemplating the mess on the floor. Strewn clothes, gnarly pizza crusts and a half-eaten packet of Tim Tams were definitely where I'd been.

And what did that say about me?

It said my life was in disarray, and I had no one to blame but myself. I mean, *I'd* chosen to become a psychic investigator. And because of that, *I'd* crossed John Viaspa, the drug lord who was set on fitting me with a pair of concrete boots. But worst of all ... *I'd* chosen not to marry some nice well-to-do boy and condemned my mother to eternal despair.

The latter problem was my current vexation since recently, two presentable and divine (and I mean *divine*) men had indicated that they'd like to court me. The world had turned inside out. The sky had fallen. White was black. Blue was pink.

I reached for the Tim Tams. Chocolate for breakfast— clearly the only solution.

As I sucked the chocolate coating off the biscuity goodness, my phone rang. It was one of my best friends, Bok the Beautiful, aka Martin Longbok, fashion magazine publisher.

''Lo,' I glugged through my chocolate.

'Tara! Are you sucking on a Tim Tam? What's wrong?'

'Nothing.' Sheesh, the guy had superpowers!

'Tara!'

'Alright … it's just … I mean … oh everything's wrong!'

Bok took a long slow breath, as if he might be about to meditate. 'OK, I have a Skype meeting with Sydney soon. So, give me the quick version.'

I rolled over on my back and noticed there was the beginning of a prettily patterned mould stain on the ceiling.

'Tar-ah!' he said impatiently.

'I broke Henry's jaw.'

'You broke Henry's jaw?'

'I did it because I thought he was cheating on Smitts?'

Smitts was our other best friend. The three of us were tighter than a plate of unopened oysters.

'But he wasn't?' asked Bok.

'No,' I said mournfully.

'Awkward,' said Bok. (I just knew he was biting the inside of his cheeks to stop laughing.) 'He's always one to hold a grudge too.'

'That's not all. I agreed to … you know … go out with Ed.'

'Out … like be his *girlfriend?* You? Thought you'd sworn off that kind of thing since the last one stole your furniture.'

'Ed was in Brisbane on a job while I was there. And we … hooked up. Like … properly hooked up.'

'The old *boom chikka*, eh. But that's good news? Right?'

'Well it might have been, but something else happened.'

'There's a third thing?' asked Bok.

'Tozzi's left Antonia … for me.'

'Oh my fucking cheeseburger! You mean rich, rugged, man-mountain, Tozzi?'

'You know exactly who I mean,' I said miserably. 'Bok, what the hell am I going to do? I'm never the girl who gets to choose.'

'Time to convene the tribunal.'

'But Henry won't let Smits talk to me on account—'

'—of the broken jaw?'

'Yeah. That.'

Smitty, aka Jane Smith, was petite and perfect in every way, and married to a guy we'd known all our lives. Henry'd always been pretty tolerant of our close relationship and some of my more dubious pastimes. But punching him in the jaw for thinking he'd cheated on her kinda crossed a line. Smitts had texted me to say she'd had to hose him down from pressing charges.

In my defence, Smitts had wound me up a bit on the whole thing. She'd got green-eyed about a woman from their past and asked me to spy on her husband. It hadn't looked too good for Henny after we'd done some surveillance, and I kind of flipped my wig when I next saw him. I mean, she *is* my bestie.

'For crap's sake, doesn't he realise you were defending her honour? He should be pleased you popped him. It shows you care,' said Bok.

I perked up a bit. 'You think?'

'I do. *Not*. You broke his jaw Tara. What were you thinking?'

'I'd do the same for you,' I said, my mood deflating quickly again.

Bok sighed in a way that told me he was about to do me a big favour. 'Let me talk to him. I'll smooth things over and set up a time with Smitts. What's good for you?'

'Sooner the better. After dinner, tonight.'

'Fine. I'll get back to you. And T ...'

'What?'

'Don't do anything until we've talked.'

'Roger that.'

I hung up and continued wall-staring for a bit. That didn't make me feel any better at all. Perhaps I should go for a run, or hit the gym? Exercise was my default mood-changer. It was a habit leftover from having played so much sport when I was younger. But somehow, I still couldn't get my butt moving.

If only Cass was here. She'd want to go to the bakery for breakfast. But my runaway sixteen-year-old flatmate had left early for her part-time job at the deli. She wouldn't be back 'til late afternoon.

My phone beeped incoming messages and rescued me from my paralysis.

Call me ASAP!

It was from Garth Wilmot, my ex-fiancé and current accountant. Garth was a supercilious, uptight, know-it-all guy whom I loved to hate. He was also dependable— above and beyond—and honest.

I was immediately intrigued. I'd known Garth for more than ten years and he'd never, *ever* sent me a message like that.

I rolled back onto my stomach, and hit his name in my contacts list.

He answered in an uncharacteristically high-pitched voice. 'Tar-ah?'

'What's up, Garth? Sock go missing? Coat hanger round the wrong way?' My standard dig at his habits didn't elicit the response I was expecting.

'Can you come over right now?'

'Sure. I guess.'

'No ... wait ... they might be watching. Meet me at

Sable's as soon as you can.'

'Who might be watching?'

'Just meet me, okay?' He sounded downright panicky.

'What's the time now?' I asked him.

'4PM.'

'Give me twenty minutes,' I said crisply. 'I'll see you there.'

'Thank you.' The relief in his voice was so out of character, I got goosebumps.

I sprang up, suddenly energised, and grabbed clean knickers, a t-shirt and shorts from my sorting bench, aka the couch, on the way to the shower. Confusing and unwelcome love-life dilemmas melted away under the drill of the hot water, and were replaced by investigative curiosity. What did Garth want? Was he in trouble? He had to be in trouble. It'd be the only reason he'd need me.

I thought back to our relationship and brief engagement. JoBob—Joanna and Bob, my parents—had been thrilled to bits with Garth being both an accountant and a Wilmot. The Wilmot's were a large well-to-do family name with roots in Canberra politics. Garth had two uncles well-placed in the Liberal party and several cousins working at Parliament House. This brought him seemingly unending respectability as far as my mother was concerned, no matter how much I argued that I didn't vote Liberal and that politics was as dirty as organised crime. Or, in fact, maybe it was just organised crime in spectacles.

But Joanna had grown up with an old-fashioned awe for local two-party politics and the monarchy, and had been devastated when I broke off the engagement.

Why Tara? Why? Rang in my ears for weeks.

In fact, the Wilmots and the Sharps had taken it far worse than either Garth or I. By then we'd worked out we drove each other crazy.

Funny thing, though, was I trusted him nearly as much as I trusted Bok and Smitts. Garth still did my tax for free, and I was his date when he had to go to work soirées and boring accountants' balls. We had the rules worked out these days. We were friends who couldn't see too much of each other on account of the fact we got quickly annoyed by each other's irritating habits.

One thing Garth NEVER did was ring me in a panic demanding to see me. Also, he'd picked Sable's, my cousin's bar in North Fremantle, to meet. It was a little out of the way for both of us, and not a place he'd normally go. When Garth did go out, he liked the after-work bars in the city where the women could afford to buy him drinks.

Adrenalin shivered me alive. Something was wrong. And now, it wasn't just my love-life.

I cut short the shower, donned my clothes, grabbed a bag and car keys and scooted down the driveway of my parents' house out to my car.

My dad was in the front garden leaning over an azalea

bush with a pair of secateurs in his hand.

I waved and pulled a face at him.

He pulled an equally tragic face back.

Dad hated gardening. That's why they had a gardener who came in once a fortnight to weed and prune. These days, he only picked up the pruning shears when he was doing penance for something, or if Joanna was planning a soirée.

I hoped to hell it was the former. Joanna's soirées were impossible to dodge and usually involved her trying to set me up with an alcohol-soaked investment banker. Bok sometimes ran interference for me, pretending to be my boyfriend—until JoBob cottoned on to my ploy and had banned him.

'Soirée?' I mouthed at him.

His nod was curt.

I unlocked my car door and leapt in. It was official—I couldn't go home for at least a week.

Chapter 2

Garth was nursing a drink and a morose stare as I entered Sable's. His aura was a duller version of its usual bright tan, his blond hair had thinned a little since I last saw him and he'd put on weight.

The bar was quiet, just a few at the pool table and some late-lunchers slouched over plates of wedges and sour cream.

I took a second to appreciate the granite benches and acid-washed walls. Sable's always looked way too clean for a drinking establishment—no grimy carpet and butt-burned wood. That was because of my cousin Crack's girlfriend—who the bar was named after.

Right now, I could see her behind the bar towelling a glass within an inch of its life. I gave her a wave and sidled over to Garth's table.

'You want another one?' I asked him.

He glanced up, surprised. 'You're offering to buy me a drink?'

I shrugged. 'Looks like you need one.'

No smart comeback just a resigned nod. 'Beer, thanks.'

'Boutique?'

'Tap,' he said.

'OK,' I said, heading over to Sable.

'Hello, Tara,' she said crisply. Her red aura flashed around her in little lightning bolts. When the colour was this bright, she was usually thinking about money.

'Hi Sable, two lagers thanks. How's business? Crack?'

'Crack's at work. He'll be here after five.'

I raised an eyebrow. Since when had my little cousin got a job? Crack was allergic to work unless it involved tyre rubber, an engine, and two-stroke petrol. 'And that work would be …?'

'With a visiting racing team. They needed an extra wrench.'

'Bikes?'

She nodded and made a funny little movement with her mouth that seemed to be caught between disapproval and pleasure. Her aura seemed equally mixed up too, pleasantly bright on one hand, but racing with agitation as well. I guess that just about summed Sable up.

'That's great news. Not Bolo Ignatius, I hope.' Bolo was an ex-client of mine who turned out to be crooked. He'd offered Crack some work back before I knew his deal.

'Team Suzuki.' She pulled the drinks like she was

milking a cow with a quick, strong and efficient grip and sat them down on the beer mat. 'No cheap drinks for family anymore. I'm trying to run a business.'

I handed her a twenty and waited silently for my change. My small-talk limit with Sable had expired.

Garth hadn't moved a muscle while I was away, drilling a hole in the wall with his stare, tapping his foot against the table leg.

'Drink,' I said, plonking it in front of him.

He drained the glass in his hand, and then took several deep gulps of the new one, while I sipped mine and watched him closely. A sheen of moisture covered his face and there were perspiration stains under his arms. Garth was not a sweater. It didn't fit with his OCD tendencies.

'O.K.,' I said. 'Spit it out.'

He looked around making sure no one could overhear us. 'What's your situation with John Viaspa?' he asked.

My stomach lurched. 'What do you mean exactly?'

'I mean, I know there's been some problems, and that Nick Tozzi pulled you out of a villa in Scarborough where some guy had you tied up. I know Viaspa has had you on a-a ... hit list. I want to know where things are at now.'

'You seem to know a lot, Garth.'

'People talk. And they can't hide things from their accountants.'

'You mean you all talk to each other ... like a Bean Counters Chin Wag Society.'

He shrugged, too preoccupied to take offense.

'Why does my situation with Viaspa concern you?' I asked.

He took a deep breath before answering. 'I've been looking over the accounts of a … friend … who co-owns a boutique in Claremont.'

Garth did not have friends in boutiques. The barber was the closest he got to retail. One of my pet peeves with him when we were dating was that he bought *all* his clothes from an online discount store. They often didn't fit, but he wouldn't pay the postage to return them. 'Which boutique? What friend?'

'A … woman …' he began.

'You've been *seeing* a woman who works in a *clothes boutique?*' I couldn't keep the incredulity from my tone.

'Can we please focus on the important thing,' he said lifting his chin.

'Which is?'

'I'll tell you if you'd stop interrupting.'

'Then stop distracting me with talk of "a woman" and get to it,' I said.

He folded his arms and leant back in his chair, jaw falling into a stubborn set. 'I can always rely on you to irritate me, can't I, Tara.'

I breathed in through my nose and tried to start again. 'OK. Tell me what's going on and I won't say another word until you've finished.'

He gave that infuriating little nod he always used when he got his own way. 'I've been helping out my friend with her accounts. I've had to be discrete, as her partner and she already have an accountant.'

'So you're checking her accountant's work?'

He gave me a look, and I buttoned my lip.

'My friend noticed some discrepancies, but she wasn't sure. So I checked for her. The business is being billed for transport costs that are nothing to do with clothes. There are invoices from a trucking company bringing stock in from Sydney and Melbourne, but no record of the inventory arriving or where it's unloaded.'

'That's crappy for your friend, but what's it got to do with me? Can't she just go to her partner, or the police?'

'Her partner is Grazia Santoro.'

I stared at him blankly. The name meant nothing.

He made an impatient noise. 'She was Grazia Viaspa.'

'John Viaspa's sister?'

The colour drained from his face as he spoke. 'Younger sister. She married one of the Santoro boys. They own vineyards in Margaret River.'

I swallowed a couple of times before I spoke. 'Look Garth, I'd like to help your friend out, but she needs to go to the police. There's nothing I can do for her other than get myself dead.'

He nodded. 'So things aren't resolved between you and Viaspa?'

Resolved? That was a quaint word in the circumstances. Why was it that my cases always led me back to John Viaspa, the big piranha in a very, very tiny fish pond? 'There's only one way you resolve issues with a man like that, Garth. He goes to jail, or his quarry takes a bullet. I'm trying not to be his quarry. After Brisbane, I need to keep a low profile. I'm sorry … I feel for her … but getting into a partnership with Viaspa's sister … it's like letting a death adder nest in your bedroom.'

He sucked in his bottom lip, and chewed it for a bit. 'That's OK, Tara. I don't want to put you at risk.'

At risk. That was funny too, really. I'd been *at risk* from Viaspa for so long now that I couldn't remember what it was like before. 'Honestly, Garth, she should think about getting out of the business. Anything tied to Viaspa is dangerous and bound to be illegal. And you want to be careful too. You don't want him hearing you've been snooping.'

If it was possible, Garth got paler. 'I think it's too late for that.'

My heart gave a painful thump. 'Why?'

'I think someone's been watching my house. I keep seeing the same car cruising past.'

I had to clamp down hard on my reaction so he didn't see it. This could just be paranoia on Garth's part. 'I can put some surveillance on your house if you like.'

His expression brightened. 'Would you? That would …

put my mind at rest.'

'I'll have to get someone else to do it though. If Viaspa is watching you and they see me, it could escalate things.'

'Fine. I trust your instincts,' he said.

'You do?' Well it really was a day of firsts.

He reached out and touched my hand and his aura warmed and brightened, splashing heat on me. 'We might be very different kinds of people, but I know you're smart, Tara. And loyal.'

Garth hadn't complimented me in years, and it sat as a lump in my throat.

Then it got awkward, so he let go of my hand and I eased back in my chair.

'I'll get someone to watch your place today for a few days. Ring me if anything changes,' I said.

'How much will it cost me?'

I rolled my eyes. 'Yeah, right.'

He smiled, his aura glowed, and suddenly the paunch and the thinning hair faded to insignificance. He still had *something* when his eyes crinkled like that.

'You should smile more often,' I added. 'Now tell your friend to consider getting out. Take it from someone who knows. Viaspa is just another way to say *poison*.'

He took my hand again momentarily and squeezed. Then he let go and stood up. 'I'll tell her.'

He waved at Sable on his way out and she stopped her glass-polishing long enough to wave back. When he'd gone, she ducked out from behind the bar and came over, scooping my glass out from under me.

'You two getting back together?' she asked. Her aura practically sizzled.

I stared at her. Sable had always been nosy.

'Garth and I are friends,' I said.

'Pretty damn friendly for friends.'

That was enough for me. I was getting the impulse to growl, so I stood and slung my bag over my shoulder. 'Tell Crack I said hello.'

She shrugged. 'Sure.'

'Later, Sable.' I said and left without a backwards glance.

Chapter 3

I sat in my car, cooling my irritation with Sable and making calls.

First was to Cass. Despite being from the wrong side of the tracks, and having a freaky love for all things goth, she'd hit it off with my snobby mother who'd helped get her a part time deli job and had been spending time teaching her to read. So much so, that she'd been accepted into a TAFE Office Management course. She told me that this was so she could run *my* office. You know, when we finally got premises, after I finally earned some regular money, and pigs had flown the Pacific in high heels.

I'd tried to explain the reality of all this to Cass, but she wouldn't hear it. According to her, she was working for me as soon as she knew how to do it.

I was more concerned that she got a proper job and her own place to live. Especially seeing as my love life was about to pick up.

She didn't pick up, so I left her a message. 'Call me

when you can.'

I ended the call and my phone rang. Tozzi's name flashed in the caller ID. I let it go to messagebank. My stomach flip-flopped as I waited for him to leave a message. He wanted to meet up, and I wasn't ready for it.

I mean, I'd been fantasising about Nick Tozzi since the day I met him. He was an imposing figure at seven feet: an ex-athlete just holding his own against good food and a diminishing exercise regime. Good looking for sure, in a kind of *man's man* way. Strong but irregular features softened once in a while by a sexy grin. Direct, charming, and such a boy still at the age of thirty-six-ish. He could be arrogant though, and sometimes his overabundance of confidence annoyed the crap out of me. But his aura was like warm caramel topping on my ice-cream. I literally melted every time he got close.

I'd learned to keep all that under control because he was married. Our relationship, though complicated, was pretty much business. Then just two weeks ago, he'd told me he was leaving his cokehead wife.

For me.

Me!

Just the thought of being responsible for someone's marriage break up gave me stomach cramps bad enough to make me sit on the loo all day. I mean … I wanted Nick Tozzi … but not like this.

So, I'd been dodging talking to him by working the end

of the Slim Sledge music tour around the south west of the state. That was done now; Slim Sledge had gone home, and I had no pressing reason to NOT talk to Nick.

Before I could summon the courage to listen to his message, a text beeped through from Bok.

Dog Beach in thirty minutes. Summit meeting.

I'll b there, I replied.

Tossing my phone onto the car seat, I sent my HT Monaro, Mona, into a spinning reverse and roared off down the coast road.

It only took me fifteen minutes to reach Dog Beach. I sat on my bonnet looking down on the wind-chopped waves and thinking summer was close. The sea had lost some of its stone-cold blue tones and was softening to more inviting greens. I was a summer person: loved the feel of warm air, the sweat on my skin and the taste of salt and sun screen lotion on my lips after a morning beach swim. I loved how the Fremantle Doctor blew up every afternoon without fail and weakened the sting of the sun.

I had a sudden deep, raw urge to be seventeen again and know nothing of John Viaspa, hit men, and dirty racing team owners. I didn't want any complications in my life other than wondering which bikini to buy, which streets to jog, and whether or not I could afford a six pack of beer or a decent bottle of wine on a Friday night.

My impossible daydream was broken by the sound of a car pulling up next to me and a door clunking open. A moment later, two enormous paws planted on my shoulders and a gigantic tongue slavered saliva across my cheeks.

'Fridge!' I hugged the great furry beast then pushed him away before he pancaked me against my bonnet.

'Down Fridgey,' said a familiarly sweet and plummy voice. Even when Smitts was at her most relaxed, she couldn't hide her rounded Euccy Grove vowels. She snapped a dog lead onto Fridge's collar and pointed sternly at him. 'Sit.'

The beast-dog lolled his tongue and grinned happily. The beach was Fridge's favourite place in the world.

I grinned at my BFF and gave her a hug as well.

She hugged me back.

We hadn't seen much of each other in a couple of weeks, on account of the broken jaw episode. I was giving Henny time to cool off and she was being the attentive wife in an attempt to wear down his fury.

'How are things?' I asked.

'Usual,' she said.

'Jaw?'

She pulled a face. 'Better than he's letting on.'

I gave a large sigh. 'He's going to hang on to this forever, isn't he?'

'Not forever. For a while though.'

'Even though I was defending your honour.'

Smitty bit her lip. 'I haven't apologised to you, T. I was

a bit crazy … you know … thinking of him with her.'

'Yup you were. But in both our defences, it looked bad. He should have told me about the surprise.'

'He should have!' Smitts agreed.

We looked at each other and burst out laughing. Then Smitts bit her lip. 'I must not see the funny side of this,' she lectured herself.

At that, I began laughing so hard, I bent double to catch my breath. Fridge, excited by my mirth, galloped off around the car a couple of times hauling Smitty with him.

Bok pulled up in his old Beemer while we were in disarray.

'What's so funny?' he said suspiciously, grabbing Fridge's lead and making the dog sit.

Smitt's caught her breath and pointed. 'Beach.'

We traipsed down the path through the dunes and as soon as we hit sand, Smitts set the beast free. He went bounding to the water, jumping and snapping at waves.

We watched for a bit before Bok spoke. He was dressed in board shorts and a tight t-shirt which showed off his lithe build. His long dark hair was pulled tight in a ponytail. If he wasn't Bok, best and most irritating friend, I would totally jump him.

'Has she told you?' he said to Smitty.

Smitts shaded her eyes from the glare to keep watching Fridge who was now wrestling seaweed. 'Told me what?'

Bok glared at me.

'OK. Nick Tozzi's left Antonia. He says he's done it because he wants to be with me...'

She turned on me, hands dropping to her hips. 'How long have you known that?'

A satisfied smile curled around Bok's lips. He loved a drama.

'Errr ... since I got back from Brisbane.'

She punched me in the arm. 'Since when do you hold out on me?'

'Since your husband exiled me.'

'Uhuh. Well ... excuse accepted. But that's great news.'

'Tell her the rest ...' Bok insisted.

'I hooked up with Ed while I was in Brisbane. Agreed to go out with him ... Be an item.'

'Oh dear fuck,' Smitts said succinctly.

I shrugged. 'Yeah.'

The three of us watched Fridge's antics for a while.

'So who do *you* want?' asked Smitts, eventually.

'How does *both of them* sound?'

'Greedy,' said Bok.

'I have the solution!' said Smitts.

I turned to her gratefully. 'What?'

'Stall them while you work it out! Give yourself time.'

I thought about it for a split second. I liked the sound of it. 'OK. How?'

'Tell Nick he has to go it alone for a bit. You can't have him leaping from her bed to yours. He needs to show he's ready for the change. Stand on his own two feet.'

Light began to dawn at the end of my love-mess tunnel. 'Course he does.'

'What about Ed?' I asked her.

'Bonk him like crazy until he finds you're far too much to handle and goes for someone his own age.'

My eyes popped. 'You think that will work.'

'Men like to think they want to do the nasty anytime, anywhere, but the truth is they don't. Three weeks of asking for more and he'll be backing off, looking for a less experienced lover. In the meantime, you get to sample the delights.'

Bok shook his head helplessly and tapped Smitty on the forehead. 'How do *those* thoughts wind up in *that* head?'

'Jeez, Bok, I'm married not dead.'

I didn't hear Bok's retort because my phone rang, and I moved away to answer it.

''Lo.'

'Tara!'

'Garth?'

'Can you come to my office? I've got a … problem.'

'Now?'

'Now!' He sounded shaky.

'Sure thing, but what's—'

He hung up before I could finish. That couldn't be good.

'I have to go, guys, something's come up,' I called out to Smits and Bok. I slipped my phone in my pocket and retrieved a Chupa Chup. Peeling the plastic, I stuck it in my mouth as they walked over to join me.

'Gotta go back and see Garth,' I explained as I sucked on the lollipop.

Smitty's eyes widened. 'T!'

It took me a moment to work out what she meant. By then it was too late. Fridge was galloping full tilt at me, spraying Bok and Smitty in shaken-off seawater.

Bam! I went down like a brick wall in a demolition.

Fridge pounced right on top of me and gobbed everywhere in his frantic search for the lollipop. I gave it up as soon as I could get my hand free and it disappeared into his cavernous mouth, stick and all.

By the time Bok and Smitts pulled him off me, I was coated in saliva and sand, with a great liberal dose of it caking my hair.

Gross!

My friends pulled me up.

'Th-th-at d-d-og!' I spluttered.

'You should know better,' said Bok pitilessly.

I tried in vain to dust the sticky sand from my clothes. 'I-s the summit adjourned?'

Bok and Smitty looked at each other.

'Play for time with Tozzi. Scare Ed off with excessive jiggy-jig,' summarised Bok.

'A plan,' agreed Smitts.

'You're both ridiculous, and I love you. Now I gotta go. Stuff's happening. Please DON'T let Fridge follow me.'

They nodded and each put a hand each on Fridge's collar.

I took my cue and bolted.

Chapter 4

Wilmot and Associates was on the railway line close to the Richview Centre, but affording Garth slightly cheaper rent on account of the noise. The office sat between a real estate company and a small antique shop. They were all closed now though, as we headed into the back end of the day.

I pulled up right in front and jumped out, patting down my gobbed-on hair.

Garth was standing in the doorway with his back to me. I saw the wreckage through the window. Filing cabinets overturned, desktop computer trashed, cups and saucers and a coffee jar shattered on the floor.

'Shit,' I said as I walked in behind him.

He turned to me his face ashen.

'You OK?' I asked.

He nodded. 'What have I got myself into, Tara? I'm an accountant. Things like this don't happen to me.'

'You've been broken into before, Garth. It could just be—'

'Not like this! This is personal.'

I put a hand on his arm. He was trembling. That stabbing sensation I got when I thought of John Viaspa returned. 'Have you called the cops?'

'They're on their way. Will you wait with me?'

The local cops and I weren't exactly bosom buddies, but I couldn't leave Garth when he was so shaken.

'Sure,' I said.

He gave me an unexpected hug. 'This is bullcrap.'

'We'll sort it out, Garth. One thing at a time. Have you spoken to your friend in the boutique?'

He nodded. 'I'm meeting her after the cops have finished. At The Dog. Can you come? Convince her to get out.'

I wet my lips. I didn't want more trouble with Viaspa. I'd only managed to stay ahead of the hitman he put on me because Wal and Nick Tozzi did a commando raid on the place I'd been held hostage. The hitman had gone to jail and the heat was on Viaspa, so his interest in me had cooled. My recent trip to Brisbane had brought me in contact with him again. Any more was likely to get me that set of concrete boots.

But it was Garth … my ex-fiancé. How do you say no to an ex who's practically blubbing in your arms? 'OK. But you have to do everything my way, Garth. Promise?'

He looked me dead in the eye. 'I promise.'

'Right, well tell the cops you have no idea who could have done this. Let them do their thing.'

'You sure?'

'If you don't want both of us dead, I'm sure. I'll tell you when the time is right to share with the blue brigade. Now steady up.'

He took some deep breaths while I picked my way through the mess.

'Garth Wilmot?'

We both looked up. Two uniformed coppers stood in the doorway. I knew them both.

'Sharp?' said the smaller of the two.

'Hello Constable Bligh and Constable Barnes.'

'What are you doing here? What's wrong with your hair?' Bligh asked, staring at Fridge's gobbed-on spots.

'Moral support. Mr Wilmot is a close friend.'

Bligh kept a very erect stance which was partly about her stiff personality and partly the fact that she was a fitness junkie. One look at her and you could see that there was a tonne of muscle on that small frame. Bligh committed a hundred percent to everything she did.

In comparison, her partner, Bill Barnes, was a roly-poly kind of cop who always had a smile on his face and a Macca's carton in hand. I liked Bill, but I respected Bligh.

'We've come to take a statement. Mr Wilmot, could you step outside with Constable Barnes?'

Garth looked at me and walked slowly past them to the pavement.

Bligh came over to me. 'Sharp?'

'True story,' I said. 'He's my ex-fiancé and current accountant. He called me to say his business had been ransacked. I came over to lend moral support.'

'And that would be because …'

'It's called friendship, Constable.'

'Don't get cute,' she growled. 'This got something to do with John Viaspa?'

'Whoa!' I said holding up a hand. 'You're jumping to conclusions. I don't know anything about this or *him*.' Never say the devil's name aloud.

She sucked in a breath and held it, giving me a searching look. 'You better not be lying to me, Sharp. You owe me the truth, remember. We'll dust this place …'

'Go for it,' I said confident that there'd be no evidence left to collect. Viaspa was mean and dangerous but not stupid.

'If not Viaspa then who would want to turn your accountant over?'

I shrugged. 'Check his client list. Or maybe it was kids.'

She looked around at the mess. 'Does this look like kids to you? It's got MESSAGE written all over it to me.'

'You're the expert, Constable Bligh.'

She stopped short of baring her teeth. I didn't want her rattling my cage because I'd stonewalled her, so I gave a bit. 'Look, honestly I don't know. Garth is as straight and honest as they come.'

'You have no clue who might have done this?'

'Garth and I only catch up now than. The "ex" thing is for a reason. He drives me nuts.'

'So you're not his confidante?'

'Far from it?'

She took out her notebook and made some notes in it. 'Well step outside and wait 'til we've photographed and dusted. Then you can help him clean up.'

'Yes sir,' I said unable to resist a parting shot. Some days my mouth had a mind of its own.

The whole statement and forensics thing took forever, and I lolled about on Mona's bonnet, checking Facebook and my email and watching the people stream in and out of the bottle shop across the road as the sun slipped away.

I should be doing what they were doing, picking up a nice bottle of Pinot Gris and settling in at home to watch a movie. In reality though, I didn't have a couch (technically I did, but it was more of a wardrobe) or a television.

I was reading an FB message from Tozzi that said *why haven't you called me?* when a deep, honey-coated voice sent me sliding off the bonnet in surprise.

'And what's your answer?'

I planted my feet in the gutter and jerked around to see if it was really him or if my guilty conscience had somehow conjured up his doppelganger.

Nope. It was him. Seven feet tall and looming bigger than that in the shadows of dusk.

'N-Nick.'

'T-Tara,' he mimicked sarcastically.

'Were you looking over my shoulder just then?'

'Backlit smartphones,' he said. 'Gotta love them.'

'What are you doing here?'

He pointed to the bottle shop. 'Just on my way there and saw Mona.'

Having a recognisable car sucked sometimes; though at least she was no longer burnt orange with black drag-stripes.

'What's going on here?' he added.

Garth was walking Bligh to the door and Barnes was packing up the camera kit. 'Garth's been ransacked.'

'And Garth would be?' He was standing in shadows but I could still see the raised eyebrow.

'My accountant,' I said defensively.

On cue, Garth saw me, waved Bligh and Barnes off, and came over. He slipped his arm around me. 'Let's go—' then he saw Tozzi's towering figure in the dark and jumped back.

I grabbed his arm to steady him. 'It's OK. This is Nick, a friend of mine.'

Garth recovered enough composure to shoot out his hand. 'Sorry mate. I think we met once before. I've had a rough evening. Bit jumpy.'

Nick stepped into the street light and by the way Garth winced, returned the shake with a bone crunching grip. 'Can see that. But you're in good hands if Tara has your back.'

My jaw dropped in astonishment. This could not be the Nick I knew, being so complimentary.

Garth slid his arm around my shoulders again. 'Yeah, I know.'

Awkward.

'I'll clean up the place tomorrow. Let's go grab a bite,' Garth said to me.

Tozzi flattened me with a glare that could demolish a building, and I extricated myself from Garth's embrace. 'Actually, Nick and I have a prior engagement, G. I'll take a raincheck on dinner.'

He looked vaguely wounded but nodded.

'What time will you be here tomorrow? I'll bring Wal to help with the clean-up,' I asked.

'7AM sound OK?'

Shite. 'Sure. We'll see you then.'

We stood for a moment in uncomfortable silence. 'Well I'm parked around the back. I'll see you tomorrow.' He nodded at Nick. 'Good to meet you again.'

'And good luck with that,' Nick said to him, nodding at the shop.

'Thanks.'

We watched as Garth locked up with a chain and

33

padlock and disappeared around the back.

'What's going on, Tara?'

I opened my eyes wide. 'With what?'

'You and the bean counter.'

'Nothing's going on,' I said. 'I'm helping out a friend.'

He clenched his fist and pounded it lightly into Mona's roof.

I stamped my foot in return. 'Tozzi, what the hell is wrong with you? Leave my car alone!'

He turned and stalked away then swivelled just as unexpectedly and walked back.

Before I could speak, he pulled me into his arms, so that his chin rested on my head.

I didn't move for a moment or two, listening to his heartbeat, feeling the power in his arms.

'Are you OK?' I ventured after a bit. I couldn't see his aura in the dark but it was buffeting me like a storm.

'I missed you, and you've been avoiding me.' He loosened his hold on me.

I eased back a fraction and looked up. Even in the gloom he had that irresistible brooding thing going: hard angles and the shadows of stress beneath his eyes. Anguish added an extra sexiness to the shape of his mouth and the darkness of his eyes.

'I-I—' The stutter wasn't a put on. I couldn't think of what to say.

'Hey, before you answer that, let's go down to the beach

and murder that bottle of Pinot Gris that I just bought.'

I frowned. 'Didn't think you liked white wine.'

'I don't. But you do,' he said lightly and strode off across the road.

He bought it for me?

I trotted after him, past the bottle shop and around the back to a parking lot. A quick scan of the cars told me there was no Porsche Cayenne or orgasmic Lambo.

'Where's your car?' I asked suspiciously.

'There.' He pointed.

A gleaming Ducati Multistrada 1200 S Sport. I knew that because my cousin, Crack, was a Ducati fanatic. I grew up watching him rebuild bikes from scratch in his bedroom. If you couldn't Ducati-speak, you couldn't converse with Crack unless you were Sable—she pretended to know nothing about bikes, and forced Crack to discuss celebrities and hair dyes. For her, he made an exception.

'You bought a bike?' I said.

'I bought a bike.' He walked over, opened the carrier, placed the wine bottle in it then unlocked two helmets from the clasp.

'You just happened to have two helmets?'

He looked at me. 'No. I came to find you. Saw Mona as I came past the bridge.'

'Smitty,' I said. 'She told you where I was!'

He didn't answer. Just handed me the dark green helmet.

Why did I feel suddenly trapped when I'd dreamed for months about Tozzi wanting to get me alone?

My phone started vibrating in my pocket. I slipped it out and checked the display. It was Ed. I got a little cramping feeling in my gut. *This* is why I was feeling trapped. Guilt!

Easing it away again, I took the helmet and put it on. Guilt or not, I had to have this conversation with Nick sometime, and putting it off would just make things worse.

He watched me secure the chin strap and checked I had it tight enough. Then he got on the bike and patted me on the pillion.

Sitting on a motorbike, even a big one, with Nick Tozzi was like trying to fit behind a watermelon perched on an orange. His huge frame encroached over half of my seat space which meant I either hugged up really tight to him or sat my butt on the rear mudguard.

I tentatively slid my arms around his broad back but as he ignited the Ducati and booted it out of the car park, I found myself grabbing tight.

Tozzi drove the way, I figured, he did most things in life, with strength, control and an edge of competitiveness that made it thrilling.

We were down the very south end of Cottesloe and pulling into one of the little car bays above the last short stretches of beach, before I could rehearse what I was going to say.

Tozzi dismounted after me and rattled about in his carrier box again. Lifting out a soft sack and the wine, he set off.

I followed him down the sandy path, lit only by an early moon and the street lights. No one swam here, it was too rocky but there was enough sand to sit on and watch the waves curling in.

Nick took a beach towel out of the sack and lay it down for us to sit on. Then he retrieved two plastic wine glasses and poured in silence.

He let me gulp down some of the alcohol while he sipped. I could feel his eyes on me as I stared out to sea. The wind had dropped, and the moon was rising. I took a handful of sand and trickled it onto my toes.

'Bet you used to do that for hours when you were a kid,' he said softly.

I glanced sideways at him. He sat on half of the towel, giving me room.

'How did you know that?' I said.

'I could just tell.'

An enigmatic answer that mystified me.

'So what happened with you and Antonia while I was away in Brisbane?' I asked finally.

He looked away, out to the dreamily glowing moon. 'She's still using.'

That was no news to me so I sat silent.

After a while, he looked back at me. 'You knew?'

'By accident. I saw her in the back room of a night club with some people.'

'What people?'

'No one I knew,' I lied. Hell would freeze over before I told him she'd been buying from John Viaspa. Last thing I needed was Tozzi on some kind of vendetta. Not when I was trying to lay low.

'Why didn't you tell me?'

'Figured it wasn't my place.'

'Your place!' he exploded. 'What the fuck is that supposed to mean?'

I became rigid with anger. 'Listen, your wife and her drug addiction is not my business or my problem. Don't you drag me down here and then ball me out!'

'But why didn't you—'

I turned towards him, coolly raging now. 'I am not your wife's keeper. And I sure as heck don't want to be responsible for more trouble in your marriage. How dare you call me out of the blue tell me you want me in your life then dump this crap on me!' I jumped up in a swirl of kicked sand and stomped down to the water. Standing ankle deep, I let it cool my feet and my fury.

My mind bubbled with a soup of emotions. I stewed on them, almost forgetting him, until his large hands descended on my shoulders.

I stiffened but he half lifted me around so we were

facing each other.

'I'm sorry, Tara.'

It was far from what I was expecting him to say, but it didn't make anything better.

'Look, I'm an arse, but give me a chance to explain,' he said.

I took a deep breath and nodded.

'I've been in love with Antonia for a long time— sometimes it feels like forever—and when I commit to something I don't take it lightly. I committed to my marriage. I believed in it. I told myself if I just gave her enough time, enough chances, enough support that she'd beat this thing but …'

'She hasn't?'

'She hasn't,' he said quietly. 'Somewhere on our journey together, I fell out of love with her. But I still care. It's hard to let go. Can you understand that? But I deserve to be happy don't I, Tara?'

I softened at his earnestness and his aura warming me. 'As much as anyone does,' I said.

He took my face in his hands and brought his mouth close to mine. 'All I know is that you make me laugh. You make me feel good instead of all twisted up inside.'

'I do?'

His answer was a kiss like no kiss I'd ever had. It was tender but raw and filled with longing that threatened to buckle my bones. I don't even know if I kissed him back.

I couldn't feel my body.

When his lips released mine I stood limply, wondering what had just happened.

'Tara?' he said anxiously. 'Are you alright?'

'I don't think so,' I said hoarsely.

He still held my face in his hands and he chuckled deeply. Warmly. 'See what I mean. There's something between us.'

As gently as he'd placed his hands on me, I pulled them away. I took a slow breath.

'I have something to say to you, Nick. And there's no right or delicate way to do it, so I'm just going to come out with it.'

He waited.

'I have st-strong feelings for you too. V-very strong.' I stumbled over the words to begin with but then they came with a rush. 'But you're on the rebound from your wife. No woman in her right mind would enter into something with you so soon. You need time to sort your head out. Time alone. See what it is you really want. Make sure that your feelings for Antonia are truly in the past.'

It looked like his lips twitched in amusement or it could have been a trick of the moonlight and shadows. 'That's very mature of you, Tara.'

'Don't mock me,' I said quietly. 'I mean it. Can you honestly say you're ready for a new relationship?'

He was silent for a bit. Shifting his feet in the sand.

Glancing out to the sprinkle of stars on the horizon.

'I want to be with you,' he said stubbornly. 'I thought you'd want the same.'

My heart gave a painful thump, and I wanted to lock my arms around his neck and demand another of those kisses. 'It's not the way these things work. You need time to heal, and we need to get to know each other.'

'How long? How long do we need?'

'As long as it takes.' I was sounding so level-headed, it made me want to laugh.

'But you'll still date me then. So we can get to know each other.'

I swallowed. This wasn't what I'd expected. *Smitts*! I screamed silently. *What now? What about Ed?*

Playing for time, I bent to flick away some seaweed that had wrapped around my ankle. My fingers hooked into it, and I gave it a good yank to fling it back out into the water.

Only it didn't flick. I felt a weight attached to it, and I peered into the water. A ghastly, pale mass with a nose and ears bobbed up at me.

'Fuck!' I yelled and jumped straight into Tozzi's arms. He staggered backwards but manned up and caught me.

'Tara!' He bent his head for a kiss, thinking I was being unexpectedly passionate.

I thumped him on the shoulder before he could fix his lips to mine. 'Get back!' I shrieked in his ear.

He stepped from the water onto the sand with a giant stride and deposited me alongside him, holding me steady so I didn't overbalance.

'What is it? You're shaking. What did I say?'

'N-not you. Th-there!' I pointed to the water.

He peered around me cautiously. Then he stepped forward and dabbed at the mass with his foot.

It bobbed and nudged closer, the hair intermingling with the weed.

'Shit,' he said. 'It's a body.'

'A d-dead body.'

He fumbled in his pocket for his phone, shone the torch onto the floater.

I forced myself to look. It was a guy in a suit. Though his skin was puckered, his features were still distinct suggesting he hadn't been in the water overly long.

The wave began to recede taking the body with it.

'Grab it!' I said.

'It's a dead body,' said Tozzi. 'You grab it!'

I glared at him. 'Jeez, Nick. We can't let it wash back out to sea.'

His look told me he very easily could.

I made an angry noise and stomped into the water. The corpse's hands were tied together with rope. I grabbed them, closed my eyes and pulled. At first nothing happened so I pulled harder.

Without any warning, the resistance lessened, and I staggered backward until I overbalanced onto the wet sand.

'Tara,' said Nick in a strangled voice.

'What!'

'Look.'

I opened my eyes. I was holding the corpse's arms, pulled straight out of the jacket sleeves and off the body. That shouldn't happen. Arms don't just come off. But there they were, glistening with salt water and blood...

'Yeeooowww!' I threw the limbs away onto the sand and sat there panting, trying not to puke.

Tozzi swore loudly and in a way that penetrated my shock.

'Ring the cops!' He threw me his keys and phone and waded in, grabbing the arm-less body by its waterlogged clothes.

While he wrestled to bring it to shore, I moved further up the beach and got my own phone out. I rang the first cop number I could find in my directory: B for Bligh.

'Sharp?' said the Constable on the third ring.

She had me on caller ID? 'B-bottom of R-Rosendo St. D-dead body in the water.'

'What? Tara, explain yourself—'

'Can't! Going—to—be—'

I hung up and threw the entire contents of my stomach into the hollow I'd just dug with my feet.

My vomit-induced tears took a minute to clear then I kicked sand over the mess and stood up. Tozzi was still struggling against the pull of the water. He was sprawled above the waterline with the mound of body across his legs, lying in the shallows. I could see, like the hands had been, the corpse's feet were tied.

'Tara,' he called out.

'Yeah, Nick?' I answered anxiously.

'You should know … this date sucks.'

Chapter 5

I would have called him on that, but the sound of an engine and brakes had me scanning the car park behind us. A patrol car pulled in and I had a bad feeling I knew the two figures inside: not Bligh and Barnes as I was hoping, or even Greg 'Whitey' Whitehead, a cop I'd known since school.

'Shit!'

'What?'

I ran down to Nick. 'It's Cravich and Blake.'

'I'm not following you,' he said, tugging the corpse by its leg now.

'They were part of the raid on Coke Road last year. They would have strip searched me if Bligh hadn't interrupted them.'

'That's illegal without a policewoman present.'

'Yeah.'

He let go of the body, took my hand and squeezed it. 'You okay?'

'Please don't leave me alone with them,' I whispered.

His hand squeezed tighter. 'Are we good?'

'Barring dead bodies and dodgy policemen ... we're good. But this ... conversation we started, let's finish it some other time.'

In the moonlight his face looked as pale as mine felt. I might have pulled a dead guy's arms off but he'd wrestled a water-logged corpse from the sea. Dead guy cooties were all over him and I bet, like me, he was desperate for a shower.

Before he could answer, torches were criss-crossing the sand and glancing off our faces.

Blake called it in before either of them spoke to us. Cravich poked at the body with a pen then crouched down in front of me, flashing his torch up in my eyes.

'Tara Sharp.'

'Constable Cabbage,' I said, unable to help myself.

He frowned and gestured to his right, past a man-made rock wall that had been put there to fight sand erosion. 'Step into my office.'

'Why over there?' Nick growled at him.

'Mr Tozzi. I believe we've met before. From your previous experience being interviewed, you should know that we prefer to speak to witnesses individually.'

Nick got up. He towered over Cravich and made no attempt not to. 'I want to be able to see her.'

The policeman stiffened. 'Are you attempting to

obstruct an officer of the law, sir?'

'I want to see her when you're talking to her,' said Nick impassively.

Suddenly, I wished I hadn't said anything about the strip search. This was going to blow up into something ugly. Tozzi's voice had an edge to it that I didn't like.

'Everything alright here. Constable?' asked a voice from behind us.

Fiona Bligh had approached silently from along the beach. She was in jeans and a windcheater, a cap on her head. Off duty, but cool as a cucumber.

'Just about to question the witnesses.'

'Right,' said Bligh. 'I'll take Sharp, you take her friend.'

Cravich glowered but nodded.

Bligh grabbed my arm and frog-marched me along the beach out of earshot.

'What the hell is this?' she said with heat.

I freed my arm and put my hand on my hip. 'This is Nick and I having a private conversation on a public beach and having a body wash up by our feet.'

'That's it?'

'That's it,' I said. 'What do you think? I murdered the guy and then waited until he blew up like a whale before incriminating myself by calling it in?'

Bligh breathed in sharply. 'Don't get smart.'

I ran my hand through my hair. 'Honestly, Fiona. This is horrible and I have no idea who the body is. Nick and I were down here sorting out some personal issues.'

'He's married isn't he?'

I shrugged. She could talk to Tozzi about his marital status.

'I'll take that as a "no comment",' she said.

'Thanks for rescuing me from Cravich and Blake. Those two ...' I trailed off, not able to say what I really thought.

Bligh sighed and got a notebook out of her pocket. 'You're a trouble magnet, Sharp. OK. Let's take it from the start. What time did you arrive and when did you first notice the body ...?'

We went over my recount for about twenty minutes. I could see Cravich going through the same process with Nick.

By the time Bligh had decided she was satisfied, a white van and an unmarked car had pulled up next to the patrol car.

'Detectives are here. You'll need to hang around a bit longer,' said Bligh.

We re-joined the others then Bligh, Cravich and Blake went to confer over the body waiting for the cavalry, leaving Nick and me alone for a moment.

He pressed his giant warm hand into the centre of my back. 'You OK'

'No. You?'

'Not really.'

The detectives had arrived and were heading towards us, waving their torches around like searchlights.

Minutes later we were separated and questioned again, and by the time they said we could go home, it was close to midnight.

We trudged up to the motorbike, which was now surrounded by cop cars and a forensics wagon. Tozzi handed me the spare helmet without a word and we sped back to Garth's office.

Mona sat forlornly outside under a streetlight. I got off and watched while he strapped the helmet to the back. He gave me a curt wave and was gone.

So much for clearing the air between us.

I should have gone home, but Ed lived only a few streets away and my hands were shaking with delayed shock. Autopilot took me over the bridge and down a right hander, braking to a stop outside a set of villas.

Refusing to overthink it, I grabbed my bag, got out and buzzed his intercom.

It took a while but he eventually answered.

'It's Tara,' I said simply. 'I need to come in.'

He released the front door and I took the stairs two at a time, suddenly gripped by a desire to get inside some-where safe *with* someone safe.

'What happened?' he asked as I bowled past him.

'I need a wash,' I said. 'I'll explain after.'

He nodded sleepily. 'Spare towel behind the door. I'll

be in bed.'

My state of mind was so scattered that I barely noticed how he only wore boxers and tousled hair. 'Thanks.'

He moved to kiss me on the head but I stepped back.

'I'm wearing *eau de dead guy*. Not until I've showered.'

The sleepy look left his face almost instantly. His lips parted in surprise and concern and a crease appeared on his forehead.

I ducked away from him and into the shower where I blasted myself with water as hot as I could stand and lathered the soap like it was bubble bath. I also contemplated that the only person who ever put a frown on Ed's face was me.

Towelling off hard, I returned to the bedroom.

There was nothing terribly fancy about his apartment though it was clean for a young guy—cleaner than mine— and pretty orderly. He had a couple of rubber plants in pots by the window and a Lyn Hammond acrylic hanging on the wall above his bed. She was his favourite artist and was fast becoming mine.

He'd spent his first big pay cheque on the painting and had it shipped in from Sydney. It was an impressionistic sunset over low hills, all in dark blues and oranges. Moody and deep. We'd spent over an hour just staring at it before he'd got out the hammer and drill to hang it.

Ed was propped up in bed right now, a delicious fore-ground to the strong Hammond colours and brush strokes above. Though the artist tended towards landscapes, I bet she'd paint Edouardo in a flash.

'Tara?' The frown was there making him look older than his twenty years. I wanted to smooth it away.

'Better,' I said. 'And planning on being shiny.'

The frown disappeared as he cocked an eyebrow. 'How so?'

I dropped the towel and walked slowly to the bed. He lay there watching me, not moving as I lay full length alongside him.

He let me peel the sheet back and run my fingertips from his thigh to his chest. 'Am I allowed to participate in getting shiny?' he said with a slight breathlessness.

Tears welled and were stinging the back of my nose looking for release but I refused to let them fall. I lowered my head, so that I could run my tongue along his ribcage and my fingers drifted down between his thighs.

The combination of actions had an electric effect on Ed and I suddenly found myself underneath him, our faces level. Dark eyes stared at me with intensity.

'After this … you will tell me what happened tonight,' said Edouardo.

'I will.'

Satisfied, he lowered his weight on me and I felt his anticipation against my stomach. With his first caress of my breast, I closed my eyes and forgot everything.

We dozed for a few hours afterwards but Ed wasn't letting me off. He woke me around 6AM with a strong cup of tea and some toast and jam.

I tried burrowing under the sheets but he stripped them from my clenched fists, sat the plate of toast on my bare rump and the tea on the bedside table.

'I've got an early call. Be out of the shower in a few minutes.'

I slid my hand around to retrieve the food, pulled the sheet back up and plumped the pillows behind me. My clothes lay at all parts of the compass and a bottle of lubricant lolled on its side, dribbling stickiness onto the carpet. We'd used that, I recalled, in my last attempt of the night to out-sex Ed. My plan had failed because he was looking bright and beautiful this morning while I resembled something Fridge had dug up in Smitty's back yard.

Just then he came out dressed in a spectacularly well-cut suit. Pale mauve shirt and matching tie. His aura was a glowing aquamarine with rosy hues at the edge, except when he was tired. Then it turned to a soft azure. Right now, it was practically sparkling aqua.

'That was an epic night,' he said.

'How do you do that?' I demanded grumpily.

'What?' he asked leaning over to peck me on the lips.

'Look like Matt Bomer after no sleep?'

He blushed, which made me feel bad and also kinda turned on. Ed was still the sweetest guy. The industry hadn't jaded him yet. How long, I wondered, before it did?

'What's the job anyway?' I asked changing the subject.

'That swimwear spread I did for Martin got some attention. I got another gig from it.'

'With Bok?'

'No, with Armani.'

'You mean an Armani house shoot?'

The blush again. 'They wanted beautiful beaches. And we do have the best in the world. A bunch of them flew in from New York and Rome yesterday.'

'Which label?' I said it to be conversational. In truth, I knew there was a bunch of Armani labels but had no clue of the difference between them.

'Prive,' he said.

'Cool.'

'Yeah. Very cool. Now,' he said. 'Your turn.'

'Oh ... that was ...'

'Tara!' He cut me off before I could start mentally editing. I'd promised Ed I'd share a bit more and stop trying to protect him from my job. In his words, *stop treating me like a kid*. So I took a deep breath.

'I was talking to a friend down on one of the South Cott beaches last night. We were standing near the water and a ... body washed up.'

'What ... like a ...'

'Dead body. Yeah. Just banged into my leg.'

'Shit. That's heavy. I hope you didn't ... know the

deceased?'

'No. He wore a suit. Looked like … any guy really.' The tears I'd fought back last night snuck up and ambushed me. I began to sniff. 'I-I tried to pull him out of the water and his a-arms came off.'

Ed stiffened. 'Like right … off?'

'Yeah. Someone must have hacked at them. His jacket sleeves were holding them in place.'

'Both arms?'

I lifted my head up and gave him a tear-blurred, wobbly nod.

He bit his lip and pulled me close again. 'Sweetie, no wonder you've been in shock. You should take it easy today. Stay in bed. I'll be back about three.'

As tempting as it sounded, I had to check on Garth, and Hoshi Hara, my mentor, was expecting a visit. I'm fine,' I said brushing the tears away. 'Just needed to think about something else last night.'

'Did you … *we* do that?' he asked tentatively.

I kissed him on the cheek and the chin and the ear. 'We sure did.'

He leaned into me like a puppy nuzzling his owner. 'I'll call you when I'm through.'

He got up, straightened his suit coat and grabbed his wallet and keys from the dresser. With a quick blown kiss, he was gone.

Chapter 6

Garth was at the back of the office sorting through an upturned cabinet when I arrived. He looked up and smiled when I knocked on the door jamb.

'Glad you're here. There's someone I want you to meet.' He got up. 'Jasmine!'

A figure appeared from the back room. Jasmine was thin, dressed in a loose but expensive shift, hair upswept and wearing immaculate make-up. She reminded me of a younger version of my Aunt Lavilla, without the daring glint in her eyes. In fact, she looked pale underneath her foundation and her eyes were swollen as if she'd been crying. Her aura was a sea of wild pale blue wisps, bleeding at the tips.

I walked through the mess and held out my hand. 'Hi, I'm Tara.'

Her return handshake was lukewarm and a bit limp. I didn't put too much stock in that because of what was happening in her life.

'Can I take you two to coffee so we can talk?' said Garth.

Garth shouting me coffee? Could that be? 'Cake as well?'

He pursed his lips and nodded.

'Great!' I said. 'Let's go!'

We walked across the little railway bridge, past the supermarket, butcher, and militaria antiques shop to the Book Café. I went with Garth to the counter to pick out my cake while Jasmine reclined with distracted elegance at a table by the window.

Garth nudged me. 'Beautiful, huh?'

I was eyeing the plum and cinnamon cake, and couldn't help but agree with him. 'Delicious, I'm betting.'

The nudge turned into a jab. 'I mean Jasmine.'

'Oh,' I said feeling faintly disappointed. Plum cake appealed to me much more than she did. 'S-sure, Garth.'

He made his *disapproving* noise and gave his *disapproving* stare. 'I don't need you to appreciate her. I just need you to talk her into getting out of this partnership.'

I glanced up and narrowed my eyes. 'That's why you're taking us to coffee?'

His face fell in on itself like he might cry; only, Garth would never blub in public. 'She won't listen to me—' He broke off while we ordered and waited for the counter guy to move away again. 'I'm scared for her, T. After last night, I'm scared for me too,' he finished in a whisper.

'How the fuck do you think involving me will make things any better? You have any idea what's been going on in my life the last few months.' I took him by the arm and pulled him in close, so that my lips were right to his ear. Dimly, I was aware that Jasmine watched us with pursed lips, but I didn't care. 'You know that Viaspa put a hit on me not long ago. The guy he paid is in jail now, but for all I know the contract still stands.'

I felt him tremble. 'You mean …'

'Yeah, I mean, that standing too close to me might get you shot!'

'You should go to the police.'

I gave him a look. 'Don't preach to me about what I should do if you want my help.'

He licked his lip and swallowed. 'OK.'

Okay? He must be shaken up. Garth never gave up on anything without an argument.

'You're … are you … safe?' he asked.

I shrugged. 'No. Maybe. I honestly don't know. But I'm not going to spend my waking moments obsessing about it. I'll talk to her, but then I'm out Garth. OK? It's up to her.'

He nodded. 'Thanks.'

The guy returned with our order and we carried it over to the window table. Jasmine took a sip of her skinny flat white while I gulped my latte. Garth stared unhappily into his short black.

I allowed myself a large mouthful of the cake—plum is so divine—before I broke the silence. 'I'm not one for beating around the bush, Jasmine. Garth tells me you're in a business partnership with John Viaspa's sister?'

She froze, coffee cup halfway to its saucer. Permitting herself a quick irritated look at Garth, she placed it down without spilling a drop. 'I'm sorry?'

I took another couple of bites of plum heaven. Her frayed aura told me she was stressed, and I knew I should be more patient than I wanted to be. 'This break-in at Garth's office is no accident. He told me that you and he found some discrepancies in the bookkeeping at your work. Next thing his office is trashed. I don't know John Viaspa's sister, but I know him. This is just his style. And it's a warning. Believe me, if he thinks you're putting him or his empire at risk, there are no safe rocks to crawl under.' I thought about what had just transpired in Brisbane—the whole US gang thing—and added, 'Anywhere.'

It was a long speech for someone who'd rather be anywhere else but having to mention the name of the devil out loud.

'But Grazia—my partner—is not like that,' she said in a quick, clipped tone.

I gave her my flattest most pragmatic stare. 'Then who exactly *is* she laundering money for? Her butcher?'

'I … I …'

'Jazzy please. Tara knows these sorts of low-lifes and what they can do. You have to get out.'

Well thanks for that Garth!

She looked from me to him then her mouth twisted in misery. Garth was right, she was very attractive; funnily enough, much more so when she had a real expression on her face, not her practised haughty fake thing.

'I can't. We've got the summer collection arriving this week and a huge fashion parade to put on at the Hilton. Even if I wanted to, I can't walk away right now. Not until after Christmas at least.'

I sucked on the cake fork. 'So, if you go to the cops with this, all your assets will be frozen while they investigate.'

She nodded. 'My reputation as well and everything I've worked for. If the media gets hold of it, I'll never live down the stench.'

'But they're *laundering* money.' Garth said it softly so that no one else could hear but each word was a like a soft punch.

Tears glinted in her eyes. 'I wish you'd never found it.'

Garth's wounded look made him look so vulnerable that I felt like I'd just seen his bare butt.

Right about then I had an idea on how to get them both to leave me out of it. 'There might be another way.'

Two sets of anxious, hopeful eyes fixed on me.

I took a deep, deep breath. Garth was super-straight,

so he'd never go for this. He'd say no then I'd be in the clear. 'Before I go on, you have to understand that nothing about this will be lawful, and therefore I can't take any ownership of the outcomes.'

Garth flinched and Jasmine blinked like a big ol' owl.

'Tell us?' she whispered.

'Maybe I can find something you can use? Something which will make your partner agree to letting you go with minimum fuss, and keep your pocket and reputation intact.'

'You mean blackmail?'

'Leverage,' I said firmly. 'There's a difference.'

'Stop right now Tara,' interjected Garth. 'I won't have talk like this. You're compromising us.'

I grinned inside and ate the last mouthful of plum yum. 'Fair enough. But I don't think I can help you then.'

Garth nodded primly and clinked his teaspoon against the sides of the cup as he stirred in more sugar.

My phone buzzed and I excused myself to check my messages, walking over to the bookshelves by the door. It was Hoshi asking me to call by, but I also noticed a missed call from an unknown number.

Garth and Jasmine were having a whisper argument, so I took my time and called the number back.

'Eireen Tozzi speaking,' said the frightfully snobby voice at the other end.

'Eireen? It's Tara Sharp. Did *you* call me?'

'Young lady, I think you should visit me immediately,' came the rather superior command.

Crap. Eireen was Nick Tozzi's pocket-sized, nail-polish lacquered, upswept-bee-hived mother—the only person in the world who truly *TRULY* terrified me. '*Me?*'

'Shall we say this afternoon at three? I'll have the girl put the Doulton out.' She promptly hung up.

I stared, mouth open, at my phone and my stomach twisted into a bread plait. A summons from Dowager Tozzi. That could not be good.

Before I could sink into fearful imaginings, my phone lit up with another unwelcome number; Bon Ames, man-mountain-range, and scary biker.

I answered, thinking how strange my world was that even speaking to a badass bikie seemed infinitely more preferable to a tiny, eighty-year-old Euccy Grove widow.

'Bon? This is unexpected,' I said.

'Where are you now?'

'Umm … in a café in Claremont. Why?'

'Come out to the clubhouse. I'll text through the address.'

'*Your* clubhouse?'

'Call me when you're outside. I'll let you in.'

'But I have plans today.'

'Cancel them.' His tone was gruffer than I've ever heard it and for the second time this morning someone hung up on me. *Jeez.* This couldn't be good either.

Garth and Jasmine had their heads together still. I stalked over to them. 'I have to go. Something's come up. Nice to meet you Jasmine.'

'Tar—' Garth began, but I didn't wait to hear the rest. I had to deal with whatever Bon Ames and the Western Cheaters wanted and get back in time to see Eireen Tozzi.

Garth and Jasmine's woes had just faded to white.

Chapter 7

Mona and I hadn't had a decent spin out to the 'burbs in a while, and it was good to be on the road. The traffic on Great Eastern Highway was light and I got a quick run out Midland way.

My car, my stereo, fresh air blasting in the open window: who needs a convertible when you've got a 70s Monaro with wind-down windows?

Mona had survived her orange and black spray-paint incarnation, courtesy of a cheap job by a guy called Bog, and was now back to a more original metallic brown thanks to the pay cheque from my last job. I felt a tad more anonymous these days which was definitely a plus.

I should have used the drive time to contemplate the Tozzi/Ed thing but my mind refused to go there. Instead, I turned up the radio and let some indie rock freestyle me towards my destination.

It was all over too quickly though and pretty soon I was turning off the main highway and nosing through the streets of West Midland.

I wasn't sure what I expected, but my half-formed idea of the Western Cheaters clubhouse was blown to buggery. There should have been something grubby about it. Or at least a skull and crossbones ahoy on the flagpole.

I mean, it was a fortress all right, spread across three normal size housing blocks, surrounded by a high limestone wall that was impregnated in places by wrought iron railing. A palm tree or two swayed above the tops of the buildings and other than that all I could see were security cameras on every pillar, and a concrete sliding gate wide enough to fit a semi-trailer through. It looked like a modern mansion hunkering down for a siege.

I parked Mona a way up the street and walked back to the gate, feeling glad I was wearing joggers, jeans and a t-shirt, not some filmy dress with heels.

Alongside the wide concrete sliding gate was a narrower entrance with an intercom at shoulder height. It squeaked at me when I pressed the button, and I winked up at the camera angled down from above. After a few moments the narrow gate clicked open and swung inward helped by a giant, many-ringed hand.

As I stepped through, it clunked shut and I was left standing face to face with the Cheaters Sergeant at Arms.

I hadn't seen Bon Ames for a few weeks and in that time he'd shaved his head. The beard though, was longer, more ragged and today he wore a denim cut with his club emblem pressed into it. His baggy jeans were belted low on his thighs leaving space for his ample gut to expand above them. Bon Ames was huge but he wasn't soft. I imagined anyone driving their fist into that gut would break their fingers.

'Ames,' I said in acknowledgement.

'Sharp,' he nodded. 'This way.'

We crossed a forecourt where four or five bikes and a light blue tray-back were parked. I caught sight of two large houses a short distance apart, several garages, a swimming pool and a big BBQ area under a rotunda. Whack a golf course alongside and I could have been at the Royal Pines golf resort.

'Doing it tough out here,' I said casually.

I got the expected grunt as he pushed open the front door to the bigger of the two houses. The door had WCMC in fancy copper letters riveted to it, and they shone.

The door made such a heavy clunk as it shut behind me that I had a momentary flash of being locked in here forever. I looked around and took in the two pool tables, long jarrah bar, chairs and couches, a bunch of doors off a corridor, and a stairway. It was like you'd expect of a large Mandurah holiday house but more open plan and stinking of weed and beer.

There was an older woman in a singlet and tattoos behind the bar and two sallow young bikers drinking from coffee mugs at one of the tables. The guys eyed me suspiciously but the woman didn't bat an eyelid, wiping the glasses in hypnotic movements as if she was counting each stroke.

Bon Ames pointed to the stairs. 'Meeting's up there?'

'M-meeting?' I stopped dead in my tracks. 'What meeting?'

Bon Ames rounded on me, his eyes slightly shifty. 'Club's got a job for you.'

'What?' I tried not to squeak but failed miserably.

He breathed slowly in and out like he was being patient. 'You owe me Sharp. Remember?'

'But ... now ... right away ... I mean we only ... I only owed you ... like ... three weeks ago.'

His expression became very flat. 'Shit happens.'

'What if I don't want to do what you want me to do?'

The stare stayed absolutely the same but a corner of his mouth kinked in a nasty grin. 'You're not that stupid.'

I suddenly wished I was back in the coffee shop with Garth and Jasmine.

He pointed. 'Up.'

I forced my reluctant limbs to climb the stairs and followed his instructions to turn hard left into a room that was the same size as the one below it but was set up with a boardroom table, a bunch of laptops, a radar detector, a short-wave radio and a bunch of other electronics that I couldn't immediately identify. It could have been the

66

business hub of any legitimate white-collar operation except for the two-way and the hard-core types lounging about with their feet up on the table.

Each one of them wore their club insignia either on their t-shirt, their cut, or on belt buckles large enough to use as weapons. They all had face piercings and beards except for the guy who sat at the head of the table. He wore black jeans and an unbuttoned, collared shirt. His only piercing was in his ear and he was clean-shaven with brown hair cut to his shoulders to look messy. He might have been Rob Thomas's twin. The WCMC tattoo peeping up from under his shirt collar was the only giveaway that he might be something other than a cute muso.

Maybe he was their business manager?

'This is her,' said Bon Ames gruffly and that looked to be the extent of my introduction. I wished I'd thought to ring Wal and ask him to come for the ride. Even if they hadn't let him inside, he would have known I was here. Right now, no one in the world did. Maybe that heavy, letter-shiny door would stay closed on me forever. Or maybe they'd just bury me in the garden.

Getta grip! Getta grip! 'Hi,' I said.

No nods to my greeting, just a lot of suspicious stares.

'Siddown,' said the young clean-shaven one. His voice was cultured but sibilant as if he smoked heavily. I noticed that one of his eyes was brown the other green.

Disconcerting and fascinating.

'I'm good,' I said staying right where I was, wondering if the pepper spray was in my bag.

He nodded and grinned at the others. It was a cheeky, attractive smile laced with something treacherous. His aura wasn't quite like any I'd seen either. It was black and gold like a tiger stripe, and bristled out from his body. At the roots though, close to his skin, there was a warm golden glow. There were so many layers to his body energy, I didn't know which one to read first. Or which one was the prevailing tell. Maybe it changed as he did? All I knew for sure was this dude was one unusual person.

'Ames says you'll do for us?' he said quietly.

I swallowed and nodded, 'I guess so. Long as I don't have to kill anyone.' Did that sound like a joke?

One of the other bikers laughed and farted wetly. The guy next to him shoved him off his chair and suddenly they were all bagging each other, swearing and rolling around like little boys trying to get attention.

'Shut the fuck up,' said Clean-shaven in a clipped voice.

As soon as he spoke, Bon Ames pounded his fist on the table hard enough to break the building in half. The rest fell silent and surly again like someone had taken their toys.

'I apologise for my colleagues. We don't often host women in the boardroom.' He put both elbows on the table, and pressed his hands together in a steeple. His fingers were tanned, strong and lean. He wore a gold club-insignia thumb ring on one and a black-stoned silver ring on the other.

I shrugged and decided to go with my usual direct approach. No point in letting these guys think I rated them. 'What do you want me to do? I've got places to be.'

He smiled and his face became so attractive I almost forgot that he was … whoever he was.

'One of our … associates, has inconveniently drowned. We believe you've already met him.'

A moment of blank and then my eyes widened. 'The guy on the South Cott beach? You knew him?'

'We had certain business dealings with him and would very much like to know what happened. Because the nature of his demise is sensitive, we'd like you to look into it for us. It wouldn't do for us to be seen in some of the places that questions need to be asked. Mr Ames thought you might be able to help, and in that way, clear yourself of your debt to him … to us.' It was a quaintly formal little speech.

'Oh. What kind of places?'

'*Your* kind of places Ms Sharp.'

I nodded slowly, assuming he meant the Western Suburbs. 'And what if I don't find out anything useful …?'

'Then we'll renegotiate your favour to us.'

'Fuck aye,' said one of the beefier guys wearing a sleeveless leather cut.

Bon Ames gave him a quelling look and Beefie snarled in return. Their auras banged about like two air bags released by a crash. Suddenly I was very anxious to get out of there.

'Fine. Well, I'll nose around. I'll need some details of course,' I said.

'Mr Ames will be your contact. He'll give you what you need to know.'

I stepped back. 'Fine. I'll be going then.'

Clean-Shaven got up and strolled around the table to me. He was about my height and now he was standing close, I could see his shoulders were wide in the way of a conditioned boxer and his green eye was the colour of a tropical sea. His aura brushed up against mine like it was a stray tomcat and I was a friendly leg. Mine responded by rubbing back.

It threw me for a moment. I hadn't expected to come here and find someone whom my aura fancied.

A step back.

He held out his hand. 'I expect you'd like to know who you're working with,' he said softly.

I reached back and accepted the handshake automatically. 'Sure. Yes.'

'Jake Stranger, President of the Western Cheaters.'

The President? Well blow my stereotype out of the water. He looked more like a daytime public servant/night-time jazz muso than a bad-ass biker. 'Oh.'

'I'll show you out.' He put his hand on my elbow and gently turned me to head down the stairs.

I moved quickly to get ahead of him and leave the derisive laughter and suggestive noises that erupted around the table, behind.

He caught up and kept pace with me. When we reached the fortified door, I waited for him to unlock it. He only partially opened it, so that I had to brush close to him to get out. I hesitated and thought about how best to handle the situation. He was attractive but I didn't go for male power plays.

He waited, watching to see what I'd do. Smiling. His aura was smearing itself against mine. His fringe had fallen across his eyes.

'Jacob?'

The president of the WCMC looked through the open door to the outside. A young woman about my age stood just outside the doorway, waiting to come in. She wore biker chic: jeans, tank top, a studded belt and big hoop earrings. Her hair fell long and liquidly black around her shoulders, partly covering her tattoos.

She was beautiful—like the girls you saw posing across Harleys in bike magazines. But her expression was sour. I guessed immediately that Jake Stranger was her man, and she was sensitive to him flirting.

Jake's aura became hard and prickly as she pushed her way in, elbowing me in the ribs and thrusting her fist into his side. He didn't flinch at the body punch but his eyes narrowed.

She turned her stare to me, venom leaking from every pore. 'Who's she?' Her fist came up. 'I swear to God, Jake if you're screwing some snotty bitch in here behind my back—'

Right about there I had enough. I didn't like being called a bitch or accused of sleeping with a guy I'd known for fifteen minutes, so I took her fist in my much bigger hand and shifted it out of my face. She was smaller than me and slight, despite an enormous pair of fake boobs and a scragger's attitude.

'I'm here on business and I'm just leaving. Keep your personal shit *out of my face*.' With that I gave her my best game-day shove, sending her stumbling backward across the room into the waiting arms of Bon Ames. He folded one enormous tree trunk forearm around her waist and lifted her off the floor. She hung there like a child, kicking.

Jake, grinning again, held the door open wider.

I gave him the briefest, haughtiest glance as I stepped through, expecting to see some embarrassment or at least discomfort. To my dismay I read a flicker of admiration.

My anger turned to disgust. Time to get out of this place and never return.

As I scooted up the road to my car, I prayed that the police weren't doing surveillance on the clubhouse. I didn't need *this* dubious association tarnishing my already questionable reputation with them.

I think I was going to miss Fiona Bligh being on the beat. She seemed to be the only thing that stood between me and chaos at times.

I keyed the car open and got in. Before I could start the engine, the sliding concrete gate of the WCMC opened and a motorbike shot out and along the street to where I sat: Bon Ames in full leathers.

'Follow me,' he said.

I had to scramble to get Mona out into the traffic on the highway before I lost him. He headed east along Lloyd Street for about ten minutes then took a right-hand turn and a few more twists until we ended up around the back of the brickworks. His varying pace and route suggested he thought someone might be following us and was taking care to lose them.

When I pulled up alongside him, he said 'wait here' and roared off.

I chewed my nails for a bit and pondered how long I should give him before I left. It was a deserted, creepy part of the world and I didn't feel right.

A few minutes shy of me leaving, he returned, pulled over, turned the bike off and got in the passenger side.

He was sweating and seemed to be heavily preoccupied. I waited for him to speak.

'Thing I like about you Sharp is that you don't prattle,' he said finally.

Like? I blinked. 'Are you going to tell me why we're here?'

'Got some word as you were leaving that the club was being watched. I had something to give you that didn't need prying eyes.'

'Cops?'

He shrugged. 'Drug squad.'

Oh great! Cold sweat washed over my skin.

'Why did you ask me to come there then? We could have met somewhere else.'

'Call it insurance. And Jake wanted to meet you. It's harder for us to go out in groups these days.'

'The anti-biker laws?'

He nodded and I wanted to slap my head for being such an idiot. They knew they were being watched and they incriminated me by having me visit. It was another way to keep me in line. *Jeez.* What was I getting into? 'What is it?'

'I need you to remember most of this.'

'Uhuh?'

'The dead guy is Bernard Romeo.'

I knew the name. 'The real estate guy?'

'We need you to find out where he'd been in his last twenty-four hours. You need to do this before the police do.'

'What's his connection to the WCMC?' I asked.

Bon Ames gave me stony face.

'I guess if I find out what he's been doing that question will answer itself.'

'Maybe,' said Bon Ames. 'And if you do, you'd best forget it right away. Shame if you washed up like he did.'

I became very still. 'Are you threatening me?'

Stony face again.

I thumped the steering wheel. 'Well that's pretty fucking crap.'

'You do this for me. I'll protect you.'

'And then we're done?'

'Then we're done.'

I took a deep, settling breath. 'I'd better get on with it. The cops are already half a day ahead of me.'

Bon Ames reached into his cut pocket and brought a little black USB. 'This will help.'

I took the memory stick and fingered it.

'We didn't want to risk the drug squad pulling you over outside the clubhouse and frisking you.'

'Gee thanks.'

He opened the car door and hauled his bulk out. 'Not a problem.'

Chapter 8

I had just enough time to go home and change my jeans and t-shirt for a dress and sandals to keep my appointment with Nick's mother. Eireen Tozzi didn't understand the term 'casual wear'.

Cass was in the flat, reading cookbooks my mother had loaned her. Weird how she and Joanna had found a common interest. More than once I'd found them huddled over the *Barefoot Contessa Foolproof* at JoBob's kitchen table.

'Hey!' I said.

'Hey.' She looked up at me from an old hardcover of the Golden Circle Cookbook. 'You didn't come home last night.'

'I got caught doing surveillance on a job for Garth. You didn't call me back.'

She shrugged.

'I thought you had work today?' I asked.

She shut the book. And I suddenly noticed that her

eyes were swollen and red. 'There was a thing at the deli.'

'What thing?'

She stared at the ceiling. 'My mum turned up this morning. She was shouting and stuff ... so they sent me home.'

'Your mum?'

'The original crazy fucking bitch.'

'Cass!' It was an automatic reprimand. 'Don't talk about her like that.'

She screwed up her face. I hadn't seen that look for a while, and I didn't like its reappearance.

'It's true! She accused me of stealing money from her last week. How could I? I haven't been home since the day she kicked me out. She's so fucking paranoid. It was probably one of her junkie boyfriends.'

'Cass!' I squatted down beside her and touched her arm. 'Listen—'

She flinched so violently I withdrew. 'What's wrong?'

She looked away. From this close I could feel her trembling.

I grabbed her wrist and slid up the loose sleeve of her top. There were fresh scratch marks all down her upper arm.

'Your mum did this?'

She shrugged. Then nodded. 'Like I said, she's crazy. I should have just smacked her.'

I took her chin and moved it so she had to look at me.

'But you didn't and I'm proud of you. Nothing to be gained from doing that.'

She blinked and I could see the tears coming.

'But I promise you, I won't let her ever hurt you again,' I finished.

Saying that to her, cracked her resolve. The tears couldn't be stopped then. They wracked her body and she sobbed in my arms until she was spent.

My heart twisted up while I patted her back. I'd never known the full story of the night Cass had left home. We'd met briefly while I was doing surveillance out her way. She'd been perfecting her delinquency style, hanging out with a bunch of bored teens at the railway station. She helped me out, getting closer to a suspect than I could and reporting back. On the spur of the moment, I gave her my designer rip-off handbag as thanks.

She was clearly the one with the brains in her group of friends, which she proved by finding my house a week later and asking me to take her in after she'd had a monumental fight with her mum (dad MIA and sister in jail on drug offences). She'd arrived at Lilac Street wearing black torn tights, black worn make-up, a baggy black dress, and clutching the handbag.

'Listen. I've got to go visit Mother Tozzi now. Come with me. Safety in numbers. The woman's a terrier.'

She sat up and ground her fists to her eyes to dry them. 'Nick's mum? Can you wait while I shower and change?'

'Sure. Make it quick though. I'll be upstairs raiding the fridge for us. Wear pastel.'

She gave me a watery grin. 'Can I borrow something?'

I gave her the thumbs up. 'Back in ten to collect you,' I said.

I left her rifling through my clothes and scooted up past the swimming pool to the back door of my parents' house. It was open as usual and my mother, Joanna, had her head in a cupboard, cleaning it.

'Is that you, Bob?' she called.

'Mum you really should snip the back latch. You never know who could walk in,' I chided her.

'Don't be ridiculous darling,' she said, emerging red-faced, clutching a large casserole dish. 'This is Euccy Grove. I know everyone five streets in each direction. Besides, I have you and Cass out there to protect me.'

'Speaking of Cass, Mum, I need to talk to you.'

'Oh?' She put the spray and wipe down on the kitchen breakfast counter and came around to the table. 'Sit.'

I slumped down into the chair.

'Why is your shirt all wet,' Joanna asked, sitting opposite me, smoothing out the tablecloth.

I bit my lip. 'Cass's mother paid her a visit at the deli this morning. Caused a scene. Scratched her up. The Marios sent Cass home afterwards.'

'What do you mean "scratched her up"?'

'Her arms are all scratched. Fingernails I guess.'

Joanna's smooth, well creamed and beautifully aged face crinkled into a look of horror. 'She *hurt* her?'

I nodded. 'And accused her of stealing. I think we might have to do something about it.'

Joanna thumped the table scaring the hell out of me. Her aura—normally a steady turquoise—began to bubble like a hot spring.

'How dare she?! I will not tolerate this. Youth Services must be informed. The police! She must not be allowed to go there and treat Cassandra so poorly. My goodness if I'd been there—'

'Mum!' I said loudly, interrupting her outburst. 'I agree and I've assured Cass we won't let it happen again. But anger won't help her. She's got enough of her own.'

Joanna shut her mouth abruptly. 'Of course, dear. That's very sensible of you. What shall we do?'

My heart skipped a beat. My mother had just asked for my advice?

'Ummm … umm … well I'll take her out with me now and get her mind off it. Perhaps you could go and see the owners. See if you can talk them down on firing her. As soon as I have a moment, I'll call the Department for Protection, see if I can find out where they stand on keeping her mother away from her.'

'Hmmmm … yes dear. That's a good idea.'

I could see Joanna's mind ticking over on something. But I didn't have the energy to go there right now. I still had Eireen to survive and the day already felt like it was a week long.

'Fine. Let's talk about it again when we know where we're at with the deli.'

Joanna leaned across and patted my hand. 'You're a kind girl, Tara.'

I swear I nearly fainted. In my twenty-seven years on this earth, my mother had never called me a 'kind girl'. 'Flakey', yes. 'Scatterbrained', yes. 'Ungrateful', yes. But KIND GIRL? Was she sick? I surreptitiously checked her aura. *No.* As bright as ever. No tell-tale white patches of disease.

I got up and walked over to the fridge. Time to leave before anything else weird happened. A girl can only handle so much! 'Mind if I do a food raid?'

'Not at all, dear. Take what you need. There's half a pavlova left from dinner last night. It needs eating.'

My jaw fully dropped. But I grabbed the pav and headed for the flat before I woke up from this incredible dream.

Cass was showered and dressed in a pale lemon dress of mine that was a little too long and just scraped the top of her Doc Martens. The coupling of light lemon crepe and badass, dusty leather came off quite well, but I didn't know what Eireen would think. Whatever the case, if

Eireen Tozzi's attention was drawn by Cass's wardrobe choices, then it would be 'off' me.

We walked the long way around the block to Tozzi's mum's mansion.

'How are you feeling?' I asked Cass.

'Alright.' She shrugged. 'You know what's weird? I was pleased to see her at first.'

'She's your mum,' I said. 'We love our mums, even if we don't always like them.'

She shot me a sideways glance. 'Love?'

'What did she want?'

Another shrug. 'She said my sister wanted me to visit her in the pen. But I think she just wanted to find me.'

'Well she's seen you now. That'll be the end of it.'

Cass bit her lip and broke off some jasmine vine as we turned into Eireen's driveway. She twirled it in her fingers then began breaking it into little pieces. 'Maybe.'

I linked my arm through hers. 'Let's concentrate on surviving this, eh?'

'What's she like?' asked Cass.

'Scariest person I've ever met.'

'Seriously.'

I nodded. 'You wait.'

We crunched down the white-pebbled driveway to the highly lacquered front door. For the first time, I noticed a little crest of arms above the peephole. Maybe it was new? A lion and a bear intertwined. How apt!

A pale, skinny woman wearing a white blouse with black trousers answered the door.

'Tara Sharp to see Eireen.'

She raised a weary eyebrow that swept over Cass's Doc Martens and face piercings. 'And this is …?'

'My friend, Cassandra Loft.'

The eyebrow arched a little higher. 'I'm Mrs Brandon. Follow me.'

She led us down the familiar corridor, past the sitting room, dining room, anteroom, and finally into the sunroom. Eireen sat swamped by her floral armchair; her tiny feet encased in high black pumps, up on a footstool. Her hair looked like a stiff bird's nest made of snap frozen black electrical wire. Her eyeliner was applied in dramatic thick lines around her eyes, as though she was ready for battle.

'Tara, come here and kiss me.'

I bent over the small woman and pecked the smooth cheek. How hard to credit Nick's enormous frame was created in this petite body. 'Hello Eireen. Are you well?'

'These damn ankles of mine won't stop swelling. The doctor tells me no more heels Eireen. I tell him to "bury me in my Louboutins".'

'Heels aren't much good to you if you can't walk,' I countered.

She gave me a little push. 'Stand back, girl. Who is this you've brought with you?'

I stepped back obediently. 'This is my ... friend, Cassandra. She shares a flat with me.'

Eireen gave her a sharp-eyed appraisal that finished irrevocably on her shoes. 'What in heaven's name are those things?'

I opened my mouth to defend Cass but she jumped in ahead of me. 'They're called Doc Martens and they're chic but comfortable. Air cushioned soles. Made in Britain. Would you like to try them on?'

Eireen pursed her lips. I expected her to say something belittling but she floored me by sliding off the chair, flicking off a pump and presenting her foot.

Cass promptly sat on her butt on the marble floor, unlaced and slipped off her left shoe. She offered it to the elderly lady. It was too large but the expression on Eireen's face as she felt the spring in the cushioned soles was enough to make me look away and bite my cheeks.

After a moment of standing in the Doc, she promptly slipped the shoe off, sat down again and rang the little bell on her side table.

Mrs Brandon appeared carrying a decanter and three small, stemmed glasses.

'Aaaah,' said Eireen licking her lips. 'Here, Brandon.' She patted the side table.

'Will there be anything else ma'am?' said Mrs Brandon with a hint of weariness.

'Order a pair of Doctor Marty's for me,' she said

pointing at Cass's feet.

'Ma'am?'

'You know my size Brandon. Call Betts and have them delivered straight away.'

Mrs Brandon blinked at Cass, who was holding the tried-on shoe in her hand. 'These ones?'

'Yes. Yes. Now get on with it.'

Brandon's expression was worthy of a billboard, but Eireen didn't notice. 'You. Pour the sherry,' she said to me.

I went from biting the inside of my cheeks to chewing my lips as I tipped the amber liquid into two glasses. 'Cass is only seventeen Eireen. None for her.'

'Nonsense,' said the tiny woman. 'I drank Chianti every night when I was fourteen. I insist.'

I hesitated. 'Look, I really thin—'

'It's alright Tara,' Cass interjected. 'I've drunk a lot worse than Mrs T's sherry.'

Eireen's head swivelled between us and she gave a chuckle. '*Mrs T*, I like that. Bring this girl to visit me again.'

I swallowed and chewed harder on my lip as I poured a third drink with less in it.

Eireen made an unintelligible toast as we held our glasses up, and promptly polished hers off. She gave a small ladylike burp then pointed to one end of the sunroom. 'Now you go in there shoe girl. I will speak with Joanna's daughter alone.'

Cass grinned at me and nodded then sauntered through the door into what I knew was the library.

Damn. So much for my plans of not being alone with Tartar Tozzi.

'Come here.' She directed me to her footstool, moving her feet a fraction to make room.

I swigged some sherry and poured her and me another before I complied.

'What can I do for you Eireen?'

I knew I sounded terse, but nerves were getting the better of me.

'My son tells me he is in love with you.'

I choked on the liquid in my mouth and coughed it up into my hand.

She waited and watched me while I tried to regain some composure. Then she went in for the kill. 'I tell him, he is married, and must make it work. He tells me he has tried, but she is a bad girl. She does bad things. So, as a mother who loves her son must do, I tell him, "get rid of her".'

I raised an eyebrow and held my breath.

'The skinny one, I mean. He must get rid of the skinny one to make way for you. Two women I will not tolerate. Capisce?'

'Capish,' I managed to gasp out.

'Now you tell me what you intend for my son? You be a bad girl and I speak to your mother. My Nicky has already had bad.'

'I'm … I'm …' I tried to think of something but my mind had emptied into a gaping void.

Eireen didn't let up though. 'Good stock you come from—better than the skinny one, but you dress like a boy sometimes and you are so big. Too big for a girl.'

'I-I …'

'You want children? You must want children too, or I tell my Nicky you are no good. I am older now. I must see my grandchildren.'

'Eireen! That's none of your business!' As soon as the words were out, I wanted to take them back.

La Tozzi placed her glass carefully on the side table and drew her cardigan around her. Her expression set into so indomitably imposing that I wanted to crawl under the couch. 'You will have children with my son! Yes!?'

I licked my lips several times. 'If … if you say so.' It came out in the lamest of lame whispers.

'Good. We understand ourselves.' She picked up her sherry and gargled it down. 'Shoe girl come back,' she called out.

Cass reappeared, her eyes bright and wet like she'd been laughing hard enough to cry. I glared at her but she wouldn't meet my eyes.

'Now, it is time I watch my programmes. You go, but you come another time. Bring shoe girl.'

I stood up on slightly shaky legs. 'Eireen,' I ventured.

'This conversation will stay between us won't it?'

'Tch,' she said and waved me off, as she reached for the TV remote.

I gritted my teeth and turned to leave. 'Come on,' I said to Cass, 'best get out of here before I commit a crime of passion.'

Chapter 9

The walk home was a reversal of fortune. Cass spoke soothingly to me as I stomped along feeling angry and put upon.

'Don't sweat it,' she said. 'She didn't say you had to have kids right away.'

I shot her a filthy look. 'Is that supposed to help?'

Cass's cheeks were flushed holding in her laughter. Seeing that didn't help my mood.

I accelerated to my fastest walking pace until she had to jog to stay with my longer strides. She was puffing hard by the time I strode down the driveway past the birds.

Joanna was standing there feeding Brains an almond.

'Hello girls,' she said. 'I'm glad you're back.'

I was in no mood to chat and planned to walk on by, but the odd tone to her voice made me pull up and turn around. 'Mum?'

'Mrs Sharp?' asked Cass, picking up on the same thing.

Joanna slowly, gently leaned her head against the cage.

Her aura was shredding little bits of blue from the edges.

'MUM! What is it?!'

'Your Aunt Liv, Tara. She's had some kind of … episode. Her heart … We need to go straight to the hospital.'

Aunt Liv is my *family*. I mean, of course she is, she's my aunt, but Liv has a *very* special part in my heart. She'd embraced my idiosyncrasies when my mother could not and had a totally egalitarian view of the world that I adored—the socialist socialite with more than a little bohemian barmy to make her perfect company. I LOVED Liv with my heart and soul.

'Of course,' I said. 'I'll drive us. Where's Dad?'

'He's playing golf. I've left him messages but he never checks his phone.' Joanna staggered a little, like she might faint.

Cass grabbed her arm. 'I'll come and sit with your mum in the back seat.'

I nodded. 'Thanks.'

Together we walked Joanna back up the driveway and sat her in the back of Mona. Cass scrambled in alongside her.

'Tara, the house is unlocked, and I need my purse, and leave your father a note, and—'

'It's OK Mum, I've got it,' I said and raced across the lawn to the front door. I grabbed Mum's purse off the sideboard then stopped and pulled out my phone and rang Wal.

'Boss,' he said. 'What's news?'

'Wal, it's Liv.'

His light tone changed. 'Tell me.'

'She's in Sir Charles Gairdner Hospital's emergency department. Her heart I think, but I'm not sure. We're on our way.'

He hung straight up on me. I expected he would. Wal loved Liv as much as I did. More, possibly.

He was standing outside the Emergency double automatic doors when we arrived, smoking a rollie and chewing his fingernails.

'Wallace,' Joanna acknowledged as she swept past with Cass on her arm. My mother didn't approve of Wal and Liv's liaison, but she wasn't one to quibble in a time of crisis. It was something I liked about her.

I followed more slowly, waiting for him to stub out his cig and walk with me.

'What do you know?' he rasped out.

'Nothing more than I told you,' I said. 'We got home and Joanna had just got a call from the hospital. I rang you and we came straight here.'

'But I saw her yesterday. We played cards.'

Nothing fazed Wal. He'd roadied for every big rock band that had been through the city in the last thirty years, and plenty of the smaller ones too. He'd seen accidental overdoses, suicides, scaffolding injuries, burns ... and taken it all in his stride. Right now though, his mouth was pinched tight, and his complexion was white.

As we walked along the long white-lino corridor, I thought about how today had been full of *unexpecteds* and *firsts*. Like something was wrong with the magnetic spin of the earth.

I felt as skittish as an animal in an approaching storm.

Chapter 10

We got to see Liv two hours later when they admitted her to a hospital room for an overnight stay. She was sitting up in bed, hooked up to three blinking machines and sipping tea.

'Sis,' said Joanna from the door. 'Oh, sis.'

She rushed across to Liv's bedside and grasped her free hand.

Liv squeezed Joanna's fingers in a reassuring way, but her eyes went straight to Wal, who stood next to me.

'Don't fuss, Jo. It's just a small turn. The doctor says I need to change my diet. No more cream cheese with my caviar. Red wine instead of champagne,' she said. '*Quelle horreur*!'

Her aura looked steady, if a little washed out. I felt my body instantly relax. She was speaking, cracking jokes. She was all right.

I let Joanna tut over her for an hour before Cass and I dragged her away and left Liv with Wal.

'Call me later,' I said to him out of the side of my mouth as I kissed Liv goodbye. 'And you behave,' I said to Liv. 'You just stole ten years from my life that I can't afford to lose!'

'Thank for coming, darling,' she whispered, and I detected a wobble in her voice. Her bravado was for us, but it had shaken her.

'You need to take care of yourself better,' I said.

She gripped my hand to pull me down and return the kiss. 'Get me out of here.'

'Tomorrow,' I promised before ushering Cass and Joanna out.

It was almost dark when I dropped JoBob home. Joanna pecked me on the cheek as a thank you and muttered something about opening a bottle of wine, which I declined on account of having to go and see Hoshi.

'You going out again?' asked Cass when JoBob shut the car door.

'I need to talk to Hoshi.'

'You want company?' she asked.

'No. I want you to get on my laptop and find out anything you can about a guy called Bernard Romeo. A complete report before I get home this evening. Email it to me as soon as you're done.'

Her eyes caught fire. 'We've got another job!'

'Of a sort. Let's just say I owe a favour, and I need it to be over and done with …'

'Is it for the biker you met in Brisbane?'

I stared at her. The girl was too smart by half. 'How did you work that out?'

'You didn't say what you did this morning but you were flustered when you got back. I checked the mileage on your odometer. You'd been too far for it just to be local.'

'My odometer! Jeez. Well, Rip Van Super Sleuth you've got your own job starting tomorrow watching Garth's place.'

'What about tonight?'

'I'd planned to send Wal over but …'

'But Liv?'

'Yeah. Didn't have the heart to ask him to leave her. I'll do a couple of drive-bys later on. You be ready to start there about 7AM.'

'Ok. But Tara …' she trailed off and looked out the window.

'Spit it out.'

'I think it's time we had a paying job.'

'Amen to that,' I said and patted her shoulder.

She jumped out of Mona and walked down the driveway. Despite everything the day had thrown at her, I saw a spring in her stride. Cass was a survivor, and I was glad.

A half hour later, I pulled into the lane behind Hoshi's cottage in Fremantle, wedged the car into an old tin-roofed carport, and switched off the headlights. Mrs Hara, Hoshi's large, fierce Italian wife, didn't like me coming through the front door, so I'd taken to using the tradesman's entrance.

I found my way to the back door in the dark without tripping over his herbs and knocked on the door. Mrs Hara's chimes were tinkling in the breeze and I could smell tarragon and mint. I also caught movement in the corner of my eye: the faintest flicker of something pale, and then a sharp pain to the back of my knee.

I came around swinging but was down on my arse before I could connect with anything. A person in a bundle of flowing robes flattened me onto the deck and sat on my chest.

'Your night reading is very bad, Tara. You must get better at it. Bahahahahh …' Hoshi Hara jumped lightly to his feet and offered me his hand.

I declined and hauled myself up. 'What the hell, Hoshi?'

'Is no good that you just read auras in daytime. You must sense disturbances at night too.'

'And how do I do that?'

'Practise stillness,' he said. 'Come inside. Mrs Hara has made baklava.'

'Baklava?' I suddenly got over being aggrieved by the attack. 'Lead the way.'

I followed Hoshi into the kitchen and plopped myself down on the stool in the corner. I'd found from hard-learned experience that it was the best place for me. Everywhere else seemed to be in Mrs Hara's way. One time she even swatted me with her wooden stirring spoon for being between her and the fridge.

These days I was quite comfortable sitting on my corner stool. Only … the baklava was on the kitchen table.

'Hoshi, could you …' I began as Mrs Hara bustled in wearing a pair of lycra gym pants and a voluminous t-shirt with a Qantas airline logo on it. It was the first time I'd ever seen her in anything outside her usual floral A-line shifts and pumps. I wanted to look away, but I couldn't.

'Humph,' she snorted. 'You.'

'Bonjourno, Mrs Hara,' I said meekly. 'Martin sends his love.'

'Marty,' she beamed. 'Belissimo.'

She went straight to the bench, snatched up the roll of alfoil sitting next to the toaster and tore off a bit. Then she proceeded to wrap some honey dripping baklava into a neat parcel.

'For Marty,' she said handing it to me with a glare. Then she kissed her petite husband on the cheek. 'I go to dancing now. Your supper is in the fridge.'

With that she swooshed out of the room sucking a good amount of the world's oxygen with her.

'Will she always hate me?' I lamented to Hoshi when the door banged shut.

He shrugged. 'Mrs Hara is a strong woman. I do as I'm told.'

I blinked. 'We all do.'

'It is for the best.'

'Do you know Bernard Romeo?' I asked him, deciding to change the conversation.

Hoshi frowned. 'Dead real estate guy. Rich wife.'

'Yeah, that's it. I'm the one who found him.'

'Say what?'

I told him the quick and dirty version of that night's events, and my subsequent meeting with the Western Cheaters.

'I thought your aura was looking all messed.'

'That's probably on account of other things. The Cheaters want me to find out what Romeo did on the day leading up to his death.'

'Why so?' he asked.

'I don't know, but it seems they have ... or had a business connection.'

Hoshi shook his head. 'This not good, Tara. Bad business for you to be mixed up in.'

'Too late,' I sighed. 'Soon as I asked Bon Ames for that favour in Brisbane, I was already in trouble. It got me out of a jam at the time though ... But I need advice. How do I beat the cops to finding out what he was doing that day?

I'm already a day behind.'

'You want to find out about a man quick, you go personal.'

'You mean his personal life?'

'Yeah, yeah. You go for the personal first. Always. Police, they got their procedure. Rules to follow. Talk work stuff. Blah, blah. You go to the tender bits quick smart.'

'The tender bits, you reckon?'

He picked up a slice of baklava and squished the honeyed pastry between his thumb and middle finger. 'Juicy.'

'Right,' I said.

'Also, I got a contact at the morgue. Works night shift. Maybe he'll give you a time of death.'

'Really?' I perked up. 'That would help.'

'His name Jimmy Cricket. You call him. Say I sent you.'

'That's not his real name!'

A shrug. 'His parents lived across from the WACCA.'

I shook my head to clear away the ridiculous image of a stork flying low across the WACCA grounds to drop a baby on someone's doorstep, and jumped off my stool and gave him a hug.

'Shush, shush, Missy,' he said pushing me away. 'Mrs Hara see that she use you for sushi.'

I quickly reassumed my stool position, and copied Jimmy Cricket's number into my phone. We chatted for a little longer then I left with Bok's alfoil-wrapped treat and a notion of where to start.

I called Cass on the way to Garth's house.

'How's the background search going?'

'Boring.' She sounded tired and a bit peeved, but she was a teenager so I expected that.

'Concentrate on his social life. Look at all the photos of him online and see if you can find the drinking establishments he frequented.'

'What are you doing?'

'A drive by Garth's and then I'm going to the morgue.'

'It's not fair,' she said testily. 'You get all the fun.'

I turned up the stereo and let Lana Del Rey accompany me back along the highway to Garth's place.

He lived in a wide street that ran between the road his office was on and the highway. It was a good spot with some stately old homes interspersed with slightly meeker, refurbished, bungalows. A good, solid address but not the very best.

One time, I imagined that I'd be living there, and had wondered how I would go managing a garden in a street where people had to do that sort of thing. Of course, that never happened in the end, and I'm pretty sure Garth had a gardener to look after it now.

I cruised slowly along his street and pulled up short of his driveway, switching off my headlights. 10PM on a weeknight and Perth was in hunker-down mode. Garth's front porch light was on, and a light in the front bedroom seeped around the edges of his slatted blinds. I pictured him sitting up in man jammies, reading the business pages of *The Australian*, and checking his phone for messages from Jasmine.

The idea of him with a crush on someone was vaguely uncomfortable. It's not that I didn't wish Garth well; it's just there hadn't been another girlfriend since me, and it felt odd. I was used to Garth being single.

I chided myself for being selfish and turned my focus to the peering up and down the street and down the side of his house. All clear on the Western front. No one casing the place except me.

I took the chance to call Jimmy Cricket.

He answered after a handful of rings. 'James speaking.'

'I'm a friend of Hoshi Hara's and he—

'I can't talk,' he said quickly. 'I'm on a break in twenty minutes. Meet me outside the ambulance bay next to the big gum tree.'

'But I—' Too late; he'd gone.

I set the mortuary address into my phone's GPS and followed its clipped directions down the highway and into the city at a sedate pace. At this time of night, it wasn't going to take me long to get there. Though I would never have admitted it, the GPS voice was a teensy bit comforting. Me and dead people … well we didn't do well together.

I entered the large car park right on twenty minutes later and drove up and down the darkened rows until I spotted a large silvery gum tree on the east side near some brightly lit double doors.

I pulled into the closest parking bay and got out. Tree yes, but no Jimmy Cricket.

'Pssst!' came a low whisper.

I peered around and finally identified a head sticking out from behind the tree's wide girth.

'This side,' said Jimmy Cricket.

I walked cautiously around to the dark side and discovered a skinny, tall young man dressed in scrubs, puffing on a joint.

'You're smoking dope,' I said automatically.

'Wouldn't you, if you worked here?'

He had a point.

'You might get busted?'

'No one comes out here at this time of night except me.'

I couldn't see his face properly in the shadows and he seemed happy to keep it that way. His outline suggested largish ears and a long face.

'Hoshi said you'd be able to help me. I'm looking for a cause and time of death on one of your corpses,' I said.

'Bernard Romeo.'

'How did you know?' I said, surprised.

'Everyone wants to know.'

'As in …'

'Look,' he said. 'Let's just stick to the basics. I'm risking my job for this favour.' He sucked deeply, nervously on the joint again, and I got the benefit of the secondary smoke.

I'd never been much for chemical recreation. When you see colours around people all day long, the last thing you want is more weirdness. But Hoshi's latest bugbear that I have poor sensory acuity in the dark was true. It sure would have been handy right now to see Jimmy Cricket's aura.

'Can you help me?' I asked.

'The reports were sealed so I don't know cause of death, but the word inside is that he died about 6PM on the day he was found. His arms had been sawn and detached from his body. Hands and feet tied. Safe to say he'd been murdered.'

'So he'd only been in the water a couple of hours when he washed up?'

'Pretty stupid throwing a body in the sea just when the tide is coming in.' Jimmy Cricket giggled and then sucked on the joint again.

'Anything else you can tell me?'

He dropped the joint, stomped the end, then picked it up again and rammed it into his pocket. 'Man, I'm famished,' he said. 'Gotta go raid the vending machine. Later.'

That was the last I saw of Jimmy Cricket.

On my way home, I did another drive by Garth's. Everything was as quiet as before and the light in his bedroom was now out.

I cruised up and around the block a couple of times and then headed home. Today had been a long, stressful day, and I had a half packet of Tim Tams waiting for me.

Chapter 11

Cass woke me in the morning with a cup of lukewarm tea.

'Do I have to?' I said from under my doona when she nudged me.

'Tea. I have to go to Garth's soon. Can you give me a lift?'

I flopped the bed covers back and forced myself upright. I'd been dreaming that Ed and I were sailing a racing catamaran up past the Swanbourne nudist beach, and the sail tore.

'What did you find out about Romeo?' I asked taking the mug from her.

'Emailed it to you. Can I borrow your black jacket?'

I nodded and she rifled through the clothes on the couch to find it while I reached for my phone with my free hand.

Cass gathered her kit, and stepped towards the door. 'I'll be out of the shower in five minutes.'

Since when, I thought.

I propped on my pillow, sipped the tea and scrolled

through the email attachment. She'd given me a brief outline of him and listed all the venues he'd been photographed in. She'd also included his home and work addresses. It was comprehensive, in clear order, and she'd bothered to do a grammar and spell check. I was impressed. Cass was smart and instinctively knew how to be organised. She had so much potential in life. I just needed to break her of the idea that she should work for me.

```
Bernard Giovanni Romeo
Age: 52
Occupation: Owns Romeo Real Estate
Marital: married to Stacy Jane Bender (George and
    Phyllis Bender own the Fresh Flesh gym franchise.
    It's a national chain worth like … millions).
    Bernard took over about three years ago.
Hobbies: Travel, clothes, drinking, and snorting
    coke (according to my bullshit detector/Spidey
    sense)
Children: Armanno and Maria
Other family: Gabriel, Olivier, and Dominic: Gabriel
    married a duchess and lives on the Mediterranean
    on a bad-assed yacht. Olivier is in Sydney
    working as an account manager for a fashion
    house, and Dominic is a national pentathlete who
    lives here, but travels to Europe to compete in
    events.
```

I perused the list of bars she'd compiled and recognised about half of them. The man truly liked to gad about.

I took my last sip of now-cold tea as Cass came back in, dressed and ready to go.

'Good work on this, Cass.'

She nodded. 'I even spell checked it. What did you find out?'

'He died at around 6PM, probably not from drowning.'

'What was the morgue like?' Her eyes brightened.

'Didn't see it. Jimmy was smoking a joint outside.'

'Nice,' she said.

'No.' I pierced her with a parental-type stare. 'No drugs, Cass. Ever. Not if you want to stay with me.'

She gave a little shrug which I took as agreement. She had no money, an alcoholic mother, and a sister in jail for drugs. I didn't anticipate a problem, but I wanted her to be clear on my position.

'Cool. Let's go then. We'll drive by the bakery for breakfast.'

She beamed. 'Chocolate croissants?'

'If you insist.'

I dropped Cass at the park down one end of Garth's street complete with lunch roll, water, and a book. She said she'd text me regularly and use the loo at the café around the corner when she needed a break.

I headed home and pulled on my gym gear to go for a run, suddenly regretful that I'd agreed to Cass's choice of breakfast.

As I was pulling on my joggers, my phone beeped a text message from Aunt Liv, saying she wanted to see me ASAP.

Everything OK?

Yes. Fine. But can you come?

Around lunchtime?

Perfect. C U then

I left the flat and stopped halfway down the driveway at the bird's cage to say hello.

Brains came across immediately, but Hoo was having none of it. Galahs lived for fifty or sixty years in captivity and these two would live to double that I believed. They knew exactly what they wanted and how to get their humans to get it for them.

As I stuck my finger between the bars, Brains grabbed it with her claw and rubbed it against her crest. At the same time, Hoo started ringing his bell, demanding an almond.

I obliged Brains with one hand, and with the other reached into the treats box and fished out the two nuts.

As I held one out, Hoo leapt off his perch and beaked it from my fingers. His quick movement got Brains all fluffed up and squawking at us both. I appeased her with the second nut.

'You two really know how to get your way,' I said wagging my finger at them both.

'So I've been told,' said a voice behind me.

I swung around and found Nick Tozzi looming large behind me dressed in a t-shirt and shorts. I didn't often see him dressed so casually. The t-shirt strained across his massive shoulders and clung to the beginnings of a rounded belly.

We stared at each other for a moment or two then he said. 'We didn't finish out conversation because—'

'Dead people,' I finished.

'Yes, that.'

'I'm just out for a jog,' I said.

'I'll join you then.'

I hadn't expected that. 'You're wearing thongs.'

'My shoes are in the car. Give me a moment.' He turned and disappeared up the driveway in long strides.

I changed the birds' water dish while I thought about how to handle this. If I took him the route up Jacob's Ladder past his house, he'd unlikely have enough puff left in him to speak.

I smiled. Good plan.

I slotted the dish back in and jogged down the driveway and up the other side onto the street to meet him.

He was just tying his shoelaces as I bounded up.

'How long since you jogged anywhere?'

He lifted his head and narrowed his eyes. 'Don't you worry about me.'

'Fine,' I said. 'Let's roll.'

We jogged side-by-side east down Lilac Street in the direction of the yacht club. It was easy going for a while and downhill to the water. Tozzi was breathing heavily but managed to get some conversation out.

'How's Liv?' he said. 'I heard she'd taken ill.'

'Heard?'

'Eireen,' he said. 'Mother knows all.'

'It was some kind of heart thing. We're waiting on more tests. But the doctor says she'll be fine if she cuts out the cheese and caviar.'

'I'm sorry. I know how much she means to you.'

I shrugged. 'At least she got a warning. She was lucky. I think Wal has taken it harder than she has.'

'That's what love does to you.'

I didn't like the turn the conversation was taking. As we were only a few metres from the Esplanade, I decided to make my move.

'Here comes the tough bit. I like to go into it with a bit of a run up, like you do on a push bike.' With that I turned north and put on some speed.

I made the first half of the ascent in reasonable shape. It wasn't the first time I'd been down this route, but it never got easier. The second half was a steep summit that curled up past Tozzi's mansion and turned west again. As a kid, I'd dragged myself up and down this hill on many occasions collecting for charitable organisations. I'd hated every second of it.

For the last twenty metres shooting pains speared through both my calf muscles, and the air rasped in and out of my chest. But I knew how to push through pain, and I'd done this before.

I got to the top and resisted doing a Rocky dance. Instead, I turned and looked back for Nick. He was coming into the last gnarly bit, just past his house, and sweat sprayed off him. His breath was so loud that I had an awful moment. What if he keeled over? But he'd been a professional athlete once upon a time and breaking the pain barrier was something he'd done on a daily basis before breakfast.

With ten metres to go though, he was reduced to walking and arrived next to me bent over, his breath thundering in and out, chest heaving.

I stretched out a tentative hand and touched his shoulder. 'You OK?'

He turned and vomited over the railing into someone's rose bushes.

I took my hand away and stood awkwardly. Guiltily. I'd meant him to be out of breath, not sick. But then … this worked too.

He wiped his mouth with the back of his hands and straightened up. 'Think I'll go home and shower. I'll pick the car up after that.'

I nodded. 'OK. I'll probably be at the hospital with Liv. We'll talk later.'

He walked off without a backward glance.

I jogged the rest of the way home, deciding to shortcut.

Cass called just as I emerged from the shower.

'Everything OK?' I asked.

'Quiet. Garth's gone to work. You?'

'Tozzi and I just jogged up Devil's Elbow.'

'Nick? Jogged?'

'Kinda,' I said. 'He went home to have a shower and settle his stomach.'

'He threw up?'

The girl was so quick witted. 'Don't talk to strangers,' I said and hung up.

About forty minutes later I was sitting on Liv's bed watching her sip orange juice through a straw.

'How was your night?' I asked.

'Wired for sound. I can't wait to get home. No normal person can sleep in a hospital.'

'When will that be?'

'I'm not sure darling. I'll let you know. But there's something important I need to tell you first.'

I took her hand in mine. Liv had always given me unconditional love and encouragement. I loved my mother, but she was a different person. I suppose she'd born the responsibility of child rearing and Liv hadn't, but there was something very accepting of life in Liv's nature.

'I've found you an office,' she said.

I frowned. 'What do you mean?'

'The house on the corner adjoining Wal's flat. I bought it last week. It was going to be a birthday present to you. But in the light of things … well, I just thought I should get on with it.'

'You bought it?' I knew I was just repeating her like an idiot, but I was struggling to grasp what she was saying.

'It's an old house that's been used as a Chinese restaurant for a few years. Back in the 60s I believe one of the Boston brothers owned it.'

'The musos?'

'Yes. Goodness knows … if those walls could speak.' She smiled. 'I thought it would suit you well, seeing as you're rather crammed in at home with Cass. I couldn't bear to see that girl end up back on the street. So much potential.'

'But I can't take—'

'Yes you can, and don't argue with me. I'll be leaving it to you in my will anyway, but it'll do you more good now. If it makes you feel better, you can pay me rent for a year or so. And if you eventually decide you don't want to live there, but just use it as an office, Wallace will be right next door as a caretaker. It has a good front room, and the kitchen is restaurant grade.' She wrinkled her nose. 'But those tiny bathroom tiles. I did so hate that style. And the parking is not convenient. You have to approach from the alley behind.'

'Liv,' I gasped. 'I don't know what to say. But I will pay rent. I insist.'

'Fine. Now just say thank you, and take the keys.' She reached across to the draw in the table next to her bed and extracted them.

I trembled as I took them from her. My own house. *Mine.* It was almost too much to absorb and tears blinded me.

I hugged as hard as I could, considering she was sprouting tubes. 'Liv, this is the most amazing thing anyone's ever done for me. I just don't know …'

'Off you go now. The doctor will be here any moment to boot you out anyway. It's number 628 Stirling Highway, in case you're not sure. Go and have a look around.'

628. I knew it: could see the large brass numbers on the front of the building. The Gar Lok restaurant had been an institution in the area for years. 'Does Wal know?'

She smiled. 'Yes.'

'And?'

'He thinks I should do whatever I want with my own money. And so he should.' She blew me a kiss and waved me out the door with all the graciousness of the person she was.

I drove back down the highway in a state of shock. The urge to go and see my new place overwhelmed everything else. And it was a little early to be checking out the bars for information on Bernard yet anyway, I told myself. I had time to peek. On impulse, I detoured into Garth's street to pick up Cass.

She was propped on the slide in the park, reading her book, looking bored and uncomfortable. When she saw me, she slid down into the sand and sauntered over.

'S'up?'

'Jump in. Got a surprise for you.'

She crooked her head to the side for a moment then slid into the passenger seat. Her aura was kind of lumpy, like she wasn't quite right.

'Any action?' I asked as we glided back onto the highway.

'A stray dog in the driveway and the postie on a scooter,' she said.

'Riveting stuff.'

'I read almost fifty pages of my book.'

'Which is?'

'Office Management for Dummies.'

'You're not a dummy Cass.'

She shrugged. 'Whatever.'

I could see a mood coming on her, so I turned up the radio and began to sing.

A moment later she turned it down.

I waited. I was learning a lot about that with teenagers. You couldn't hurry their thought processes.

'I want to go visit my sister,' she said suddenly. Her body language was stiff, she was half turned away as if to protect herself.

'In jail?'

'Uhuh.'

Her sister was in Bandyup Women's Prison on drug related offences. I wasn't sure how close they were; Cass had never really said. There'd been just the two of them and their mother who I was rapidly beginning to believe was suffering an alcohol related psychological disorder.

'You want company for that?' I asked.

She swivelled in the seat to look at me. 'You'd come with me?'

'Sure,' I said. 'Though you might have to convince Joanna that you should take me instead of her. She's rather fallen for you. I'm sure she'd like to go with you too.'

'Mrs S's the bomb,' she said.

'Truly?' I raised my eyebrows. More like a bomb blast.

'You're lucky, Tara. She doesn't drink hardly or …'

She left the rest unsaid, but I knew where she was going with it … at least my mother didn't hit me. She was right. I had a lot to be grateful for.

'You find out the details and give me a date. I'll drive you there,' I said.

She reached across and squeezed my arm.

'So that book you're reading,' I said as I turned off the highway into Glyde Street. 'It might be useful.'

'Whyso?'

I veered into the first sandy laneway abutting Wal's flat and proceeded a little way down, pulling Mona into one side of a rusty roofed carport.

'Hey, where are we going? You picking up Wal? Tara?' said Cass.

I could see her getting impatient and a little anxious, but I wasn't going to spoil the surprise.

'Now,' I said. 'Do you trust me?'

She took a moment but then nodded.

'Get out of the car then.'

I covered her eyes with my sweater and led her slowly down the narrow walkway between the Gar Lok and the Health Foods shop next door.

'I can smell soy sauce and Minties,' she said.

'Hang on, Sherlock,' I said as I positioned her in front of the door and inserted the key in the lock. I'd seen a back door as well, but it felt more significant entering through the front.

It opened with a satisfying click, and I pushed Cass in front of me over the threshold.

'Oh dear,' I said.

The large front room harboured a decayed and food-stained carpet, an upturned broken table and an empty fish tank that smelled … fishy. Near the door was a long red counter with a large chipped statue of Buddha on it. Red paper shades with dangling gold tassels hung from the ceiling. I flicked the switch but only a few were working.

'What?' she said. 'You're killing me.'

I slipped the sweater off her eyes so she could see.

'Welcome to our new office,' I said.

She yelped and jumped on the spot, clapping her hands. Then she ran around touching and peering behind things. In the space of half a second, my sulky goth teen had transformed into the energiser bunny.

'Woah,' I said. 'Settle!'

'This is ours? How is this ours? We need furniture? And it has to be cleaned. But we should keep the lanterns. Where's the loo ...'

I walked over to her and grabbed her in a bear hug. 'I'm renting it off Liv. Now there is plenty of time and much to be talked about. You need to concentrate on doing well at your business course first.'

She blinked at me with slightly moist, kohl ringed eyes and took a deep breath. 'I've never seen anything so beautiful.'

I grinned down at her. 'Neither have I.'

We explored the rest of the place together. Up some narrow stairs were two bedrooms, a bathroom and loo, and a lounge area big enough for a couch and a TV. Though small, it was double the size of my flat and had indoor amenities. One of the bedrooms looked like it had been used for storage. Dry noodles lay scattered on the floor and there was a red sauce stain on a patch of the lino. It faced west, and looked out on the highway. You could hear the dull grumble of the mid-morning traffic. The other room was larger and in better condition, aside from an ashtray filled with cigarette butts on the windowsill. I walked over and looked out. The view was east to the leafy street behind and the well-to-do houses that stood in it. It was pleasant and soothing.

Perfect. But I shook myself. I'd already wasted precious time.

'I have to be at Laramie's as soon as it opens. Then get to the Cocked Dog. I'll drop you back at Garth's on the way.'

'I suppose you'll want the bigger bedroom,' she said with a sigh.

I glanced at her, startled. Cass was expecting to move in with me. I hadn't expected that. Nor had I thought about it. Had I given her that impression? 'Let's go,' I said.

She followed me out and chattered on about moving and decorating plans all the way back to Garth's, where I dropped her, before driving on to Subiaco. I'd sort that out later, I told myself. It was time to canvas Bernard's drinking holes.

A bleary eyed bartender was just opening Laramie's front door as I parked near the cellar door and walked around. The bar had a black stone façade dotted with small windows. Inside, heavy wood beams hung low over slabs of table with upturned stools on them.

I sidled up to the bar and ordered a lemon, lime and bitters. The bartender mixed the drink and set it down in front of me on a paper coaster. Moisture trickled down the side, and I drew a squiggle in it with the tip of my finger. 'Thanks.'

'Early start,' he said, as he unpacked glasses from the dishwasher.

'Actually, I was wondering if you knew this guy.' I pulled my phone out and showed him a photo of Romeo from an online article.

'You're a bit late to the party, aren't you? Cops were here most of yesterday asking questions.'

'I'm working privately,' I said. 'Just doing some background for a client.'

He looked up from the dishwasher and cast me a sharper appraisal.

'I'm not the person you want to speak to. I'm usually gone by mid-afternoon. I handle the stock inventory and open. But a shift comes on at 4pm. They know the regulars.'

'I might come back then.'

'Sure.' He shrugged and moved back to his jobs.

I opened up the document Cass had sent me and consulted the list of bars. The Cocked Dog was nearby, so was Jasper Jones'. I expected they'd be the same as

Laramie's. Then there were a bunch of nightclubs that definitely wouldn't be open. At the bottom of the list she'd left me a note.

** *Try Fresh Sally's* on Broadway.

I called Cass and she answered in one ring.

'Where the hell is Fresh Sally's?'

'It's the juice bar at the Fresh Flesh gym on Broadway.'

'That's not a bar.'

'Yeah, but his wife runs a chain of gyms.'

'Still don't get it. Why the juice bar?'

'Dunno. Just figured it would be easier to pick up at the juice bar than in a class.'

'He was married. You think he was picking up?'

'He was a guy, Tara,' she said with mild sarcasm. 'A guy with a super-rich wife who runs like a gazillion dollar business.'

'Right.' *So young and so jaded*, I thought mournfully.

I hung up, finished my drink, and hit the road to Broadway. The traffic was light, so it took less than ten minutes. The juice bar was at one end of the gym and populated by women in Lorna Jane sweatbands and Nike runners.

I asked around with no luck. If Cass was right about him picking up gym bunnies, he'd not likely do it under the nose of his wife.

A quick google located three other juice bars closer to the city, a little outside the Western suburbs. When I walked into the second one and showed the guy behind the counter his picture, I hit gold.

'That dude,' said the blond guy behind the counter mixing smoothies while he bounced to the beat of an R&B track on the stereo. His aura was a soft green, running around him like an incoming tide. 'He's that real estate guy that washed up on the beach? Yeah, he was here that day about five in the pm. I remember because the spin class finishes then. Someone told me he was the owner's husband, but that's just a load of bull.'

'You know him?'

'Seen him here a few times.'

'He did spin?'

'Not that I remember. He used to meet a girl here. His daughter, I think. He'd park his Mercedes and jump in her car. They always parked out the back behind the big skip bin. Would see them when I put the rubbish out.'

I bit my lip. 'His daughter. Right. Can you tell me what she looked like?'

He frowned, and his aura thinned into a strip of jade. 'Should I be telling this to the police? I mean, who are you?'

'Private investigator. And I'm sure the police will find you if their investigation leads them in this direction. I'm just doing a general background report for a client.'

'Sweet!' he said with enthusiasm. 'Like CSI.'

'No, that's forensics.'

'Right. Yeah. Course. 'Cept we're not meant to talk

about our clients.'

I leaned in. 'Well if it's his daughter, I already know who she is, so it's not like you'd be telling me something I couldn't find out.'

His expression lightened and so did his aura. 'If I said she was dick-stiff hot, and she drove a black re-conned Alpha Spider, late series, probably a four, that would be totally cool?'

I didn't know much about Alpha Romeos but I knew someone who did. 'It would be cool, apart from the stiff bit. That's just gross.'

He blushed and his aura began to thrum around him like it was pleased with itself. 'Sorry. It just slipped out.'

'Right.'

'Right.'

I gave him a stern look and left.

I went back to Laramie's and the others on the list, but learned nothing of use. The police had interviewed the staff and put a gag order on anyone who knew anything. I sat outside The Cocked Dog wishing I hadn't ordered that third Coke and wondering whether I should go back inside to use the bathroom, or just go home. I decide on the latter and put in a call to Crack before I started driving.

'How're they hanging?' he answered.

'They don't hang. That's the point,' I said dryly.

'Hi, Tara. Sorry about that. Misread your number.'

Again? 'I need a favour. What do you know about series 4 Alpha Romeo Spiders?'

'Well cars aren't really my thing but I know a guy who services Alphas in this area.'

'You do?'

'What do you want?'

'I'm guessing there wouldn't be too many black cars of that model in the Western Suburbs. You reckon you could find out who drives it?'

'Leave it with me,' he said.

'It's kind of urgent.'

'It's you Tara. Of course, it is.' He clicked off before I could reply.

I pulled a face at the phone and started Mona. Time to pick Cass up for dinner.

Five minutes from Garth's house, Crack called me back. I hit the speaker tab and went hands free. 'Speak.'

'You alone?'

'Yeah why?'

'This a case you're working on?'

'Yeah. Why?'

'The woman who owns the car … it's Phoebe.'

'Kenilworth?' My tone grew strident. 'You mean Premier Kenilworth's daughter.'

'Yeah, I do,' he replied softly. 'Tara, what have you got yourself mixed up in?'

Chapter 12

'Shit.'

I felt odd. Phoebe had been a couple of years below me at school. Normally you wouldn't know younger kids, but her dad was already famous then, and her mum was stinking, filthy, rotten rich from some European jewellery family.

I bumped into her one time when she was about fourteen, smoking weed amongst the ivy overhangs behind the grotto at school. I'd suggested what she was doing wasn't smart and a good way to get herself expelled, and she'd given me the finger and told me to 'fuck off'.

Her aura had been a bristling white that was marred by dark spots here and there. I might have paid closer attention, but I was ignoring my gift in those days.

'I remember her from school,' I said to Crack. 'You knew her, didn't you?'

'Yeah. A bit. And Sable did some modelling with her too, I think.'

'Don't tell Sable,' I said automatically. 'Best you don't know anything about anything.'

'You're right,' he said. 'And you keep your big fat head down in the trenches.'

'Always,' I said.

I thought I heard him snort as he hung up.

Phoebe Kenilworth. *Jeez.*

My phone rang again as I drove down Railway Parade through the back of Claremont. The caller ID flashed Cass's name. I was about three minutes from Garth's street, so I let it go through to messages.

Phoebe Kenilworth and Bernard Romeo. *Shit.* Scandal or what?

It was just after dark as I cruised past the little children's park and came up empty. No Cass.

I felt a rush of concern but calmed myself and did a full loop of the street.

Nothing.

I pulled over and called her.

She answered on the first ring. 'Where are you?' she whispered.

'Where are *you*? I've come to pick you up.'

'In the laneway behind Garth's house. I'm behind the fence post watching a guy casing the place.'

'Don't move and *do not* do anything. Even if he breaks in. Got it!'

'Yes.' She sounded a little breathless.

Cass was a bold kid, but she was still a kid: sixteen going on thirty-five.

I accelerated down the street and parked the car in the mouth of the laneway up on a shoulder of sand. There was enough room for another car to pass, but it was obstacle enough to make them slow down. I went on foot the rest of the way, resisting the temptation to use the torch on my phone.

My eyes adjusted quickly. Lights were on in all the houses as I ghosted past. Halfway along, the lane got quite a bit darker. The back yards were larger, showing the outlines of bushes close to their fence lines. I walked slowly, trying to sense sounds as well.

Garth's house should be just about—

'Tara!' A hand shot out and grabbed my wrist, sending me recoiling in fright. 'It's me,' Cass hissed quietly.

I pressed my chest where my heart had just exploded and squatted down next to her. After a moment or two, I could see the dark outline of Garth's cottage.

'Where's the guy?' I whispered in her ear.

'He's on the tin roof over the garden.'

I knew Garth's house intimately. I mean, it was almost half mine at one time. The tin roof lay over an extra car port that he'd had built at the back to park his old EK Holden under. It was his grandmother's car and now a collectible. Garth didn't part with anything that might be worth something. Once a month he kicked the engine over and hosed the outside down to keep the salt and the dust off it. The rest of the time it stayed quietly snoozing under a tarpaulin.

The roof almost connected with the main house, though it was a rough job and not something I'd rely on to carry my weight. I squinted into the dark and thought I could see a black blob atop it.

'How did you first see him?'

'Luck. I got bored watching the front so I did a big lap around looking at the houses. He was scoping the alleyway as I walked past, so I kept going. Pretended not to notice him.'

'Did he see you?'

'Yes, but I kept my head down. Then I ran all the way around to the other end. It was nearly dark, so I hid between the solo bins at the end. Just as it went dark, he came down the lane and climbed the fence. That's when I rang you.'

'Right. Well done. I want you to take the keys, go get in my car and lock the door.'

'No way,' she whispered back indignantly. 'I found him.'

'Cass, it's not safe. He could come running back out here and find us. What if he's got a knife or worse?'

'There's two of us and one of him.'

'Don't be so—'

She stirred restlessly and her voice raised a little. 'I'm staying!'

I bit my lip. We were a fair distance away. I could send her running if he jumped down. 'OK but no closer. Understood?'

She nodded, I think, and didn't further the argument.

'Where's Garth?' she asked instead.

'Work probably. Or with Jasmine.'

'Should we warn—'

I stalled whatever she thought to say by squeezing her shoulder. The blob was on the move.

We watched in silence as it crept slowly along the car port roof line then stood up.

'He's going to jump,' whispered Cass a second before the shadow leapt across onto the roof of the main house. The noise was no more than a light clunk.

'He's done that before,' I muttered. Not that I knew anything about cat burglars, but this guy didn't hesitate or stumble. 'Or he's been practising.' My stomach roiled at the thought. How many times had this guy been on Garth's roof?

'But why the roof?' said Cass. 'Seems like the hard way in.'

'Garth's office's in the loft. There's a window entry on the north side. Hard to see from the road. It's in that peaked part of the roof.'

'What are we going to do?'

I thought for a moment. 'Call Wal and have him come and pick you up. I want you to scout two blocks east and west and take down all the licence plates of cars not in driveways. I'm going to stay and trail him back when he leaves.'

'Cops?'

'Garth doesn't want them involved and nor do I unless we have to …'

'Like if someone starts shooting at you,' she said in an acerbic tone.

'Something like that. Now go. If I lose him, your intel will be essential.'

She made a faint humph noise, stood up reluctantly, and crept off along the lane. I waited until I could see her back out on a lit section of the street then I let myself in quietly through Garth's back gate.

Most people in Perth still didn't lock their back yards up, on account of being … Perth, and I knew the layout of Garth's pretty well: lock up shed on the right housing not-recently used gardening equipment and the frames of old pushbikes; remnants of a veggie garden lay in front of that; a brick paved path ran through the middle, alongside the car port, which in turn fanned into a larger paved area with some garden seats and a little statue of a cherub who peed water into a bowl. The cherub had been a gift from me, a joke really, but Garth had dutifully put it in as a garden feature, and bought a wrought iron garden setting to match.

I slid along the line of the shed and then scuttled over

and crouched next to the statue.

Nobody shouted, or hit me on the head. That was encouraging.

It seemed wise to wait there for a little bit and see if I could hear anything but after a few moments of silence, I got antsy and shifted to the side of the house that harboured the office above it.

A few more quiet breaths and then I carefully, slowly, stepped back from the house towards the side fence and peered up at the attic window under the peaked roof arch.

I couldn't see the dark blob of the burglar crouched anywhere or signs that the window was open. Where had he gone? Had he got inside already and closed the window behind him? Surely not in that space of time. Not if it was locked.

I stared at the darkened roofline and felt my skin prickle with fear. What if he was armed? Maybe I should call the police? But what if he could lead me back to whoever was after Garth?

Then I had a brainwave. I knew where Garth kept his backdoor spare key. I could sneak inside, hide, and watch to see if the burglar was after anything in particular. Then I could follow him.

I crept back across to the wall and felt my way along it to the woodpile near the back door. With care, I lifted the chopping block and felt around underneath until my fingers encountered a plastic capsule, which I broke open.

The key was cool in my sweaty palm and I made a fist so as not to drop it. Then I ran lightly up onto the back porch and let myself in through the door.

It only made a faint click as I entered. As long as I didn't stumble into anything in the dark, I'd be okay.

I stopped and listened. There was a faint rustling upstairs. Like someone shifting things around.

Drawing on my memory of the house, and aided by the faint glow of the kitchen's digital clock, I negotiated my way to the stairs then crept up them on my hands and knees. Ten up to the landing and then another five to the bedrooms. Then another five to the office attic.

When I got to the top, it occurred to me that I should have armed myself with something. Garth kept an umbrella at the bottom of the stairs. It would have been better than nothing. I wavered over going back down to retrieve it and decided the risk of making a sound was too great.

A gentle thump followed by creaking came from Garth's office. Taking a deep breath, I crawled onward to the office door. Slowly, oh so slowly, I turned the door knob and eased the door ajar. I could see nothing through that tiny sliver, and had to risk opening it further.

Just a little … just a lit—

And there he was, squatting near the desk, leaning on the floorboards with his weight on the palms of his hands.

I repressed a nervous giggle. As if Garth would keep

anything under the floorboards. That would require his lifting carpet and using tools and … *you don't know Garth, Mister,* I thought a little hysterically.

The burglar became still. Maybe I had made a noise. Or the act of opening the door—even a little—had changed the nature of the darkness or the air pressure. Or maybe he'd just had a sixth sense of my presence.

All I knew was that torchlight suddenly flashed up above my head, then dropped and settled on me peering through the door-crack.

It blinded me a bit, which meant that as he charged me I was slow to react. I got my forearm up to protect my face from his kick. It prevented a broken nose, but the momentum of the attack knocked me backwards on top the landing.

That umbrella would have been good right about now. I had to make do with rolling sideways as he went to stamp on my chest. His shoe glanced off my shoulder instead and I managed to scramble up onto my knees.

The burglar wasn't hanging around for round two. He leapt down the stairs in a few bounds and I heard him clatter towards the back door. I tried to follow at speed but ended up stumbling, rolling my ankle a little.

No time for that! I jumped the last four steps to the bottom, ignoring the pain, and chased him. I had the advantage of knowing the layout of the yard.

The burglar was on the other side of the cherub and

heading straight to the gate. Maybe he'd been scoping the place for a while. He seemed sure of his trajectories.

That left nothing for it but an all-out assault. I switched to sprint mode and exploded past the statue into a flying tackle.

I took him down heavily about half way along the paved path, in line with the window of the garden shed. The crunch of impact told me I'd regret this later, but in the moment, all I cared about was pinning him down so I could see his face. I wrestled him for a few seconds and managed to maintain the top position.

He swore and flailed and bucked underneath me. I was flung sideways and he began to scramble free, but I righted myself.

Then a light shone on his face from the side.

'Freeze or die!' said a weirdly gravelly female voice.

The burglar hesitated for a moment, long enough for me to get a glimpse of his face. Pasty skin, pointy chin, zits and mousy coloured hair that was curly on top—he wasn't likely to be on any Most Desirable lists. Not a face I knew either.

I tried to get a sense of his aura, read him beyond my brief physical impression, but the energy lines were distorted by the dark.

He bucked upward with his pelvis and knees, and catapulted me over his head, so I went sprawling onto my face. In one quick movement, he was on his feet.

I grabbed at his ankles and was dragged half upright. Enough so that he got off a glancing punch to my mouth that knocked me into the torch holder.

We got tangled and the burglar escaped into the dark.

'Tara?' The gravelly voice was suddenly much higher and squeakier.

'Cass? What the—' I rolled off my young charge and got to my feet pulling her up with me, glaring into the gloom.

'Wal and I came looking for you,' she said defensively before I could yell at her.

I touched my mouth and felt the wetness of blood. Shit. 'Wal?'

'I called him like you said. He's gone to cover the front. No wait … here he is …'

Another light flashed down the side of the house towards us.

'Wal,' I called out. 'Here.'

He hurried over, strobing us with his beam.

'Boss, you're bleeding,' he said.

'He got off a punch,' I said. 'But it's OK. Nothing broken.'

Wal put a steadying hand on my shoulder, which I appreciated. My mouth throbbed, my ankle hurt, and my tooth felt a little loose. But more than that, I was affronted and a little shocked. I don't think anyone had ever punched me in the mouth before.

'You should have waited. What if he'd knifed you? Or worse,' growled Wal.

I hid being shaken in brazenness. 'If I'd waited, I'd never have seen where he was looking. We'd never know if he was just a plain old burglar or not.'

'What was he after?' asked Wal.

'He was checking the floorboards, so I'm reckoning a safe.'

'Is there one?'

I shrugged. 'Maybe. But it won't be in the floor. Not if I know Garth.'

'You recognise the guy?'

'No. But I got a good look at his face thanks to Cass. I'll know him next time we meet.'

'You could do an identikit for the cops,' said Cass.

I shook my head. 'No cops. Not yet. They'll assume I'm involved in something. Did you take down number plates?'

'I took photos of all the cars not in driveways, on the east side of the block. Then Wal turned up and we came running because you didn't answer when we rang.'

I pulled out my phone and saw the missed calls. 'Well thanks.'

'Where does that leave us right now?' said Wal.

My shoulders sagged as a wash of exhaustion flooded over me. I'd had enough of today. 'Heading home for a shower and some food. Now that my adrenalin was fading, I was ravenous. 'Pizza. My treat. I'm starving and I've got a couple of phone calls to make.'

'We have to celebrate anyway,' said Cass.

'Why's that?' asked Wal.

'Tara and me … we're moving in next door to you,' she said.

Chapter 13

Wal took Cass home while I drove to Al's pizza parlour, taking care to wipe the blood from my lip and tighten the laces on my sneaker so I didn't limp, before I went in.

That arrangement spared me any immediately awkward conversations with Cass about moving, and gave me time to recover from my altercation. I flexed the ankle as I waited. Only a light sprain, I decided. Those always felt worse than they were.

How was I going to tell Cass she was staying with JoBob at Lilac Street without upsetting her? I mean I *couldn't* have a sixteen-year-old living upstairs from a slightly dubious investigative agency. And much as I would prefer not to have to admit it, it was dubious. I mean, I wasn't an ex-cop with strong law enforcement ties, I didn't have a private detective's licence, and I wasn't always exactly pedantically lawful.

I was just trying to get by and manage this strange ability I had. Sometimes that meant my choices weren't clear cut. And Cass needed clear cut. She was a teenager. It was bad enough that I had her out stalking cat burglars.

Guilt threatened to overwhelm me, so I distracted myself by calling Bon Ames.

'Yeah,' he said.

'Hi is that—'

'You got the wrong number lady,' he said, cutting me off.

I hesitated. He knew my voice, I was sure of it, which meant his phone was tapped, or he was somewhere he couldn't talk.

'Sorry about that,' I said and hung up.

Al called my order of a Supreme, a Meatlovers, and three lots of garlic bread, so I collected the food, feeling the flutter of panic in my belly. How did I contact Bon Ames now? I wanted the Cheaters out of my life as soon as possible. And then there was Garth's problem.

It was only a ten-minute drive from Al's to home, but I decided to call Garth and get it out of the way.

I heard background music and voices as he answered.

'Tara?'

'Where are you?'

'The Cocked Dog, having dinner with Jasmine?'

'Can you step outside for a minute?'

'Sure, hang on.'

I kept the speaker on and waited for him to find a quiet spot. The streets were quiet for early evening, but the car park at the Napoleon Street markets was crowded. Everyone must have stopped there to buy dinner. Those that could afford it. I never went there on account of the cost.

'You there?'

'Yup, I said.

I was almost at Glyde Street, and gave a glance at my new premises as I passed by. Maybe I'd leave the Gar Lock sign up. It was a good casual cover that might confuse the idle passers-by, which was likely a good thing. I didn't really want tyre kickers.

'What is it?' said Garth.

'I've had people watching your place and there's been a break in.'

'What! Where are you ...? I'll come right away. Have you called the police?'

'Whoa, settle,' I said. 'First off, the burglar's gone and he didn't take anything.'

'How do you know?'

'I was inside watching him.'

'You were what!'

'I don't want to explain on the phone. Tell me, do you have a safe?'

He hesitated and I could imagine the expression on his face: part anxious, part annoyed, part cagey. A Garth face.

'Let me put it another way. Have you kept any evidence of the thing we've been discussing at home?'

'No,' he said. 'It's somewhere else.'

'Good. Leave it there. And do me a favour, stay with Jasmine tonight. I don't think he'll come back now, but I'd feel better if you weren't there. I have to go home and get some sleep and think. We'll talk in the morning.'

I could tell he wanted to protest, but he knew that I was likely to bail on the whole thing if he didn't do what I asked.

'OK. Are you OK? Should I be worried?'

'Yes and no,' I lied. 'I'll call you first thing.'

Five minutes later I was on my bed, ankle elevated on a pillow, managing to chow down my pizza with extra pineapple and anchovies despite a fat lip and swollen cheek. Cass had transferred all the clothes from the couch onto her cot bed and she and Wal were propped on the two-seater. Wal had the pizza box on his lap, and his hand dived in regularly to retrieve the next slice. Cass had taken a couple of slices onto a plate and was picking the anchovies off.

'I'll have them,' I said.

She pulled a face. 'How can you eat them?'

'The expression is "acquired taste",' I said.

'Code for old-folk-weird,' she countered, which caused Wal to snort some salami down his windpipe.

Cass had to get him a glass of water.

By the time he'd quit spluttering, I'd eaten my share of the Supreme and was eying his pizza box.

He saw the avarice in my stare and slid the Meatlovers down behind the couch away from me.

'You wanna talk about this case, boss?' he said in an effort to distract me.

It was better than talking about the 'moving house' thing, I figured, so I told him them about Garth and Jasmine and Jasmine's link to Viaspa. Cass asked questions to fill in the bits that were new to her.

'This job on mate's rates?' asked Wal.

I sighed. 'Worse. Ex-fiancés rates.'

Wal nodded sagely. 'I had one of them once.'

'An ex-fiancée?' I said incredulously.

Wal was one black Sobranie shy of being mistaken for Russian Mafioso, despite having Irish, Scottish and Polish ancestry. He'd been a band roadie for most of his life when he wasn't working 'foreigners' as muscle for a mate or a mate's mate. He wasn't tall, just brawn with the manner of a person who didn't give a flying fuck who he messed with if the mood took him. I mean, in a fair fight, I'd even back Wal over Bon Ames, the man mountain bad biker...

I suppose as a younger guy he might have borne a slight mystique around him, though truly it was hard to imagine Wal as any other age. When I'd met him a few months back, he was suffering from untreated narcolepsy. Little did I know that months later he'd be my security chief and that my cultured and wealthy aunt would fall in love with him? Or that he'd return that love a hundred-fold. Uncle Wal he'd be, the way things were going. Whoever said that fact was stranger than fiction knew what was what.

'Her name was Janice. Hairdresser from Gosnells.'

'What happened?' asked Cass, her eyes bright with curiosity.

'Her dad had other ideas. Wanted her to marry their bean counter.'

'Why's it always the bean counter,' I said dramatically.

'That sucks,' said Cass.

'No,' said Wal. 'He was right to do that. I had nothin'. Was goin' nowhere. Can't say I like the bloke much though. Even to this day.'

'The accountant?'

He nodded.

Before I could say something about not holding that against our client, Garth, there was a knock at the door.

Wal and I exchanged quick glances. It was after 11PM. Past the time for normal visitors.

'Expecting someone?' asked Wal quietly.

I shook my head. The curtain was pulled across the glass sliding door, so it was impossible to know who it was without peeking.

'It might be Ed,' I whispered back.

'Or Nick,' said Cass helpfully.

Wal signalled for Cass to go over next to the fridge out of the line of sight. Once she was there, he pulled a knife from an ankle sheath, climbed onto the kitchen sink and carefully opened the window that faced onto JoBob's swimming pool. 'Turn the lights out, count to ten then open the curtain real quick, but not the door,' he said quietly. Then he climbed through it.

I began to sweat. Had the burglar followed me home? Come to finish the job? Had Viaspa heard I was helping Garth and sent someone to abduct me? That was stupid, I told myself. Kidnappers didn't knock.

Keeping most of my body to the side of the door so that it was protected by the wall, I reached out and threw the floor length curtain back.

There, behind the glass, stood a young guy I'd never seen before dressed in leathers and MC boots. He glanced nervously over his shoulder, like he'd heard a noise behind him.

'Who are you?' I asked politely from behind the locked door.

'Bon Ames sent me.'

'Oh,' I said. 'OK. Hang on.'

I opened the door.

'I've got a burn—' he said, reaching inside his jacket.

But Wal tackled him from behind before he got the rest of the words out—a heavy, knee hugging, bone crunching clinch that sent them both sprawling onto the floor. A second later they were wrestling earnestly. Wal had the upper hand but the young guy wasn't going down easily.

'Wal! Ssstop!' I hissed. 'He's from the Cheaters.'

Neither of them seemed to hear me, so I was forced to try and pull Wal off him. But it was like trying to separate dogs in a fight and my sprained ankle meant I kept overbalancing. Neither listened to me and all I got was a kick in the leg and an elbow in the chest.

Just as I thought about grabbing the hose from the back yard something unexpected happened to end their ruckus.

'Ta-rah!' said a piercingly plummy voice that could un-varnish woodwork at five hundred paces. 'What on earth is going on here?'

Her offended tone worked like fire blanket on their testosterone. Both men instantly stopped their wrestling, and Wal rolled off Leather Clad Guy.

'Mrs Sharp,' said Wal breathlessly, scrambling to his feet. If he'd been wearing a hat, I swear he would have tipped it.

Leather Clad Guy got up more slowly, but kept his head bowed in deference to the might of Joanna's tone.

'Wal was just showing our new employee some self-defence moves,' I said blithely into the wake of the pregnant silence.

Joanna crossed her arms. She was wearing a pale pink tracksuit and had a string of pearls around her neck as if she'd come home from some grand event and forgotten to take them off. At least, I hope that was the case. Her head was tilted to the side, her expression sceptical.

'Indeed. Well there is a time and place for such things Wallace. You're keeping poor Bob awake. Next thing the neighbours will be calling.'

'Pardon for that,' said Wal meekly.

'Sorry Mum,' I added.

She glanced around the room frowning. 'Cassandra, what are you doing down there in the corner.'

Cass emerged from her hidey hole. 'I ... err ... dropped something behind the fridge,' she said.

'What thing?'

'Oh, just a book. I put it there and then knocked it down accidentally.'

Joanna's frown deepened. 'How very odd, Cassandra. And Tara, I'm not pleased to find a young man here so late at night. Cassandra is only sixteen.'

I blushed in a way that only my mother could make me do. Normally her interfering would madden me, but right now it was fortuitous. 'They were just leaving.'

Wal nodded vociferously, and the Leather Clad Guy began to sidle towards the door.

But Joanna pinned him with a stare. 'What's your name dear?'

'Pete.'

'Well, Peter. You seem nice enough, except for those

drawings on your hands. But don't call in to the house this late again. Understand?'

'Mum!' I exclaimed, mortified.

Pete nodded nervously. He had the startled look of someone who'd stepped into another dimension without a tour guide.

'What on earth are those drawings anyway?' Joanna demanded of him.

He wet his lips, trying to summon an answer to Joanna's direct and faintly entitled question about his tattoos.

'They're religious tattoos Mrs S,' piped up Cass. 'Pete is very devout. It's a family thing.'

Joanna's expression mollified and rather ridiculously, Pete gave Cass a grateful look. The young biker seemed petrified of the Euccy Grove matron.

I wanted to stop the charade right now, but felt powerless to articulate my thoughts. Wal was acting just as impotent, holding his hands in front of him like a chastised school boy.

'Devout, you say? Not one of those strange cult religions from overseas, I hope,' said Joanna.

'Russian orthodox,' volunteered Cass again. 'Been around since ... God.'

I stared at her. Where on earth did that girl get her *sang froid*?

Cass didn't return my glance but kept a steady comforting smile directed at Joanna.

'Very well, then. I'm going up. Perhaps Wallace and Peter and I should all leave together,' said Joanna.

'It's alright Mum. I'll see them out,' I said finding my tongue finally. 'You go on up to bed.'

Joanna took one more look around the room, sniffed at my clothes piled on Cass's bed, and whooshed her pink tracksuit and pearls out of the room.

We all sagged in the wake of her exit.

'Peter?' I said when I recovered my composure.

'Pete,' he said reaching into his jacket again. He tossed me a burner phone. 'There's only one number on it. Ring the sarge tonight.'

I nodded.

He nodded. Then he couldn't help but look at Cass again. They exchanged something. No more than a look but their auras surged towards each other. I guessed he was her type. Lean and dark and looking like he might grow into someone with charisma.

'I'll go with him,' said Wal. 'Call me if you need me boss.'

I nodded, mute. My bed looked so enticing. This last little hiccough with Joanna had sapped the rest of my interest in today. But I couldn't sleep yet.

I waved Wal and Pete out. Then I limped over and locked the kitchen window and closed the horizontal blind.

'I have to make a call,' I told Cass. 'I'll be out on the lawn.'

She tilted her head to one side, and accurately assessing my mood, got about removing the clothes from her bed back to the couch, without comment.

I went outside and stood, letting my eyes accustom to the dark, listening to the sounds of Pete's motorbike growling away down Lilac Street. Wal would be walking home. He was good in the shadows.

Up in JoBob's house, Joanna extinguished the kitchen light and a few minutes later the bedroom light.

I took a deep breath and exhaled slowly. One more thing to do before my bed and I got to have that date.

I moved slowly away from the flat down to the very bottom of the garden where Joanna had a row of hibiscus against the back fence. There was a stone two-seater in front of the bushes she called Night Fire and Persephone. During the day, the flowers were an electric pink with deep purple tinged edges. Right now, they were closed up, like most of the rest of the city. I took a seat and enjoyed the peace. I should probably call Ed as well, but that wasn't going to happen.

When I was ready, I turned on the burner phone and found the one stored number. Bon Ames answered almost immediately.

'What?'

'Hello to you too.'

'Don't fuck around Sharp.'

I swallowed the dry lump that had suddenly manifested

in my throat. Should I tell him what I'd found out? And if I did, would that be enough to level my debt to the Cheaters.

'I might have something,' I said carefully.

'Speak,' he demanded.

'He spent the last hour before he died with Phoebe Kenilworth ... the Premier's daughter.'

Ames was silent for so long I wasn't sure he was still there. 'Bon?'

'Yeah.'

'Did you hear me?'

'Yeah. You did good, Sharp. Now toss the phone. If I need to speak to you again I'll send Bubba over with another burner. Meantime, scrub my number from your SIM card.'

'Bubba? You mean Pete?'

He didn't answer. Instead he hung up.

I sat for a few more minutes in the quiet dark of Night Fire and Persephone's shadows wondering where that left me. Then I went back inside the flat and locked the door.

Chapter 14

I woke up with a dry mouth and a headache. Rolling over, I saw Cass was still asleep on the fold out bed. She tended to work her way onto the top of her blankets and she liked to crook her knees up until she was curled in a ball.

I slipped my feet onto the cold lino and tested my ankle. It seemed less painful, so I tiptoed across to check on her. Her face was slack with sleep, her bottom lip jutting forward slightly. More tiptoeing took me over to my phone on the arm of the couch. It was 6.30AM. Joanna would be up and I needed to have a conversation with her when Cass wasn't around, so I headed to the main house after swinging by the loo.

The pool cover was peeled back, suggesting that someone had been up doing laps already. I yawned at the thought. Swimming wasn't my favourite pastime. A splash in the warm salty sea was fine, but laps in a cold pool before breakfast—ungodly.

Joanna was sipping tea at the counter, reading a

cookbook. I paused for a moment in the doorway. How should I start this conversation? She looked so sweet sitting there in her pale pink silky PJs, her aura slowly gently burbling around her. But the woman was made of kryptonite.

I took a deep breath and stepped into her den.

'Morning Mum,' I said and eased past her towards the coffee pot.

'Moring darling, you're up early.' She took a moment or two before glancing up from her recipe.

I poured the coffee into one of her everyday Doulton china mugs and took a sip. 'Nice flavour.'

'From a little boutique roaster in Brisbane. Arabica, they're called. Quite divine.'

'Hmmmm …' I said sipping again.

She closed the book and sat up straight. 'What is it?'

'What do you mean?'

'You're standing in my kitchen at 6.30AM complimenting me on the coffee. Something's on your mind.'

I nodded. Might as well get to it. 'Yes actually … you see, Liv's done something.'

'What do you mean? Is she alright? I spoke to her last night, and she said she'd be out in a day or so. Tara, what are you keeping from me?'

'Mum, calm down. Liv's fine as far as I know. But she asked me to call past the hospital yesterday. She told me that she's bought me premises for my business.'

'Your business?' she said suspiciously.

'My investigative agency.'

'Oh, that's what you call it?'

I let that go. 'Yes. She's purchased the old Gar Lok restaurant, near Wal's flat. It needs to be re-outfitted a bit but there are two bedrooms upstairs.'

She was still for a moment, a guarded expression on her face. 'When will you be moving out?'

'Soon,' I said. 'The next few days.'

'Very well.'

'But …'

'Yes.'

'There's the issue of Cass.'

'A Chinese restaurant is no place for a sixteen-year-old girl,' said Joanna.

'I agree,' I said. 'So … I was wondering if she could stay here in the flat.'

Joanna blinked a few times then cleared her throat. 'Why do you think that would be acceptable?'

'You said yourself, the Gar Lok wouldn't be right. And she has nowhere else to go,'

Joanna's eyes narrowed. 'You're too old to be passing your responsibilities on to me, Tara. You must deal with them yourself.'

'My responsibilities? It's not like I took this on. It just happened. What would you have me do? Call welfare? Cass is sixteen. It's unlikely they'll either be interested or able to do anything. And she can't go home to her mother.'

'No indeed! Dreadful business. Fortunately, I have managed to get her job back for her at the deli though.'

'Truly?' I felt the tightness in my chest ease. 'That's wonderful. How did you manage that?'

'I explained the situation. That the girl is a refugee and that …'

'Joanna!' I admonished my mother, my instance of pleasure evaporating.

'What's wrong dear?'

'She not a refugee.'

'She is, in a way.'

I put my elbows on the bench and my head in my hands. 'Do you know how that sounds?'

Joanna looked baffled. 'What do you mean?'

'Prejudiced, privileged, insensitive, inappropriate … take your pick.'

'Oh don't be so delicate, dear. You always dramatise things.'

I made an impatient noise. 'She can't stay here then?'

'I think Cassandra has the makings of a superior young woman, but I've done my child rearing. She's your responsibility.'

'What was all the recipe swapping about then? The chit chat?'

Her face reddened. 'Is there a law against being kind to my daughter's friends? Oh, that's right … there is…' The last was a sarcastic dig at me, for past parental avoidances.

I straightened up. 'Fine, Cass will come with me.'

'That's settled then.'

'Yes.'

We stood staring at each other from an arm's length away, and yet the divide between us in that moment was immense. I set my coffee cup down carefully in the sink, and left the kitchen quietly.

I walked slowly back to the flat, deciding the order of the day. We could move to the new offices after I'd seen Garth and talked to him about last night. I'd set Cass to packing while I was out.

I took a detour by the garage to grab my suitcase and some stored boxes from the outside storage room. When I opened the door, and inhaled the mustiness, it bought back memories of me hiding in there when I was a kid in trouble from JoBob. The broken armchair that I used to curl up on was still in the corner. The blue corded upholstery looked more faded than I remembered, and there were tell-tale signs of rat nibblings on the arms. I stood on my tiptoes and pulled my suitcase down from a stack of folded outdoor chairs. The dozen packing boxes were folded and leaning against the wall: reminders of my transitory life. I selected four. That should be enough. Cass had precious little.

Loaded up, I staggered past the birds to the flat. They squawked at me with dismay, distrustful of the boxes and

my swaying. Galahs were hardwired to flee at sudden un-
familiar movements and people staggering about loaded
up with junk.

I clicked my tongue soothingly, but they fluttered their
wings and Brains dropped to the floor, knocked down by
Hoo's flutterings.

'Silly birds,' I said gently. 'Just boxes.'

I continued awkwardly up into the back garden and
almost tripped over the doorstep into the flat.

'Rise and shine, Sunshine,' I called to Cass. 'Open the
door for me.'

I didn't get the expected groan, or any reply at all, and
dumped my load.

Inside, the bed was rumpled and empty.

'Cass?' I called.

When she didn't answer, I called louder towards the
shower and loo. 'Cassandra!'

When she didn't answer this time, an uncomfortable
feeling crept into my belly. I went inside and checked
around her bed. Her phone, the Marc Jacobs bag I'd given
her and her meagre pile clothes were gone. So was my
beach bag and the fluffy toy dog, I'd given her when she
arrived.

I ran out of the flat and back up to the house.

'Mum!' I cried. 'Have you seen Cass?'

Joanna appeared from the laundry, container of bleach
in her hand. 'What's that?'

'She's gone. She was asleep when I came up to speak to you, and now she's gone. All her clothes. Everything.'

The queasy sensation in my stomach blossomed into something more panicky. 'Do you think she could have heard our conversation?'

Joanna frowned and blinked a few times. 'Was the door open? Did you leave the door open behind you when you first came in?'

'Yes. No. I mean … I don't know.'

'Tara!'

'You're the one who said you didn't want her living here,' I replied angrily to her admonishment.

'As I recall, you were wanting to leave her here. You're the one she wants to be near, Tara. Not me.'

Joanna's flat statement gave me reason to pause. She was right. I was the reason Cass was here. I was the reason she thought she was going to grow up to be a private investigator. I was the reason …

'I have to find her,' I said.

'Yes, you do.'

'She can't have got far on foot. I'll drive towards the highway.'

'I'll get Robert to take us towards the river.'

I nodded. 'Thanks.'

Joanna frowned and looked as if she had something more to say.

'What, Mum? I need to go.'

'I didn't want to fight with you dear. I just wanted you to—'

'Take responsibility. I know. I'm about to do that.'

She shrugged and a look of mild contrition replaced the frown. 'I do like Cassandra, you know.'

I patted her shoulder awkwardly. 'I know you do. Me too.'

'Then let's find her.' She disappeared off into the depths of the house calling for my father.

I ran back to the flat, grabbed my keys, phone and bag, threw on jeans and a tee and headed barefoot up the driveway to Mona. Minutes later I was at the highway without having sighted Cass. I did a U turn and backtracked. If she was trying to avoid being seen she may have taken a less direct route. I began a more methodical search of the streets in a grid pattern. When that turned up nothing, and my calls to her cell phone remained unanswered, I rang Joanna.

'Anything?'

'No. We haven't seen her.'

'Hang on, Mum.' I checked the time on my phone.

'I have something I have to do. Can you keep looking?'

'Tara—'

'Work. It's important.'

'Very well.'

'Call me the minute you sight her. We need to talk to her together. Reassure her.'

'Yes. But I'm …'

'What?'

'I shouldn't have said those things. Cassandra is welcome to stay in the flat.'

'Well let's worry about that when we find her.'

'Goodbye, dear.'

I hung up and turned Mona back towards the highway and Garth's house. I needed to catch him before work.

Ten minutes later, I caught him about to reverse out of his driveway. Garth normally walked to work, being as it was only a block away. He must be going elsewhere.

I blocked the road and jumped out of Mona.

He hung his head out of his Jeep looking vaguely annoyed. 'Hey, I'm late for a client meeting.'

I jogged up to the driver's side and leaned in the window. 'Call them and say you're delayed. We need a few minutes.'

He squinted at me and nodded. As I walked around to the passenger side, he made a call and killed the engine.

I slid in next to him. 'Where were you last night?'

Garth blinked a couple of times and his aura expanded and changed tone in a way that told me he was embarrassed.

'I don't care if you were handcuffed and covered in chocolate in a Northbridge brothel, just tell me where you were.'

'I stayed the night at Jasmine's. She was feeling … upset about everything. Why?'

'Have you installed a safe in your office since … I … since you and I …?'

His eyes widened. 'Yes, it's behind the shelves on the wall.'

'What's in the floor then?'

'The floor? Nothing.'

'You sure?'

He frowned. 'There's a hollow in one of the floorboards. I used to use it for documents until I had the safe installed.'

'When was that?'

'Last week.'

'Had you told anyone about it?'

'Tara, tell me what's going on.'

'The burglar last night … they didn't hurry and they knew which room to go to. They were trying to lever up the floorboard and then they saw me.'

'You were *in* my bedroom?.'

I pulled a face. 'Time to move your spare key. But make sure you tell me where.'

He ran his hand through his cropped hair and licked his lips.

'Garth did Jasmine know about the hidey hole in the floorboards?'

His aura contracted rapidly and the colour intensified. 'You're not suggesting—'

'I'm not suggesting anything. I'm just collecting facts.'

'It doesn't sound like it,' he snapped.

I felt my blood pressure skyrocket. 'Look, I have other things going on in my life. Helping your girlfriend extract herself from a poor business decision by partnering with a family of vipers is not something I particularly wanted. Either answer my damn question, or sort your own problems out.'

He blanched, went to speak then pursed his lips. After letting out a breath, he spoke softly. 'I'm sorry. It's just, she would never …'

'Fine … she would never. But did she know? Possibly she mentioned it to someone else.'

Finally, he nodded. 'Yes, she did.'

'What's in the safe?'

'Two USBs.'

'Details on the laundering?'

He nodded. 'Two copies.'

'First thing, make another copy and give it to me. Then split those two up. One in the safe, and one somewhere else. Not at home. Do you have a safe deposit box?'

'No, but I can get one.'

'Maybe you should. Whatever you do, this tells us that, for the moment, you need to be circumspect. Be vague about your schedule to everyone except me, no details. Not even to Jasmine.'

'I can trust her,' he said stubbornly. 'She came to me for help remember. She's the one who's at risk here.'

I wasn't prepared to be so charitable. 'Maybe.'

He licked his lips again. His eyes flicked around as he processed my suspiciousness. 'Am I in danger, physically, I mean?'

I tilted my head. 'Honestly, I don't know. Probably not at this moment. But with Viaspa, you never know. Just take extra precautions and keep the house locked when you're inside. Put a padlock on the attic window.'

'Do I need like a gun or something?' His voice seemed disconnected, so did his expression.

'No. Nothing drastic like that. Just be extra cautious.'

'What are you going to do?'

'I'm going to ask some questions. Meanwhile you just go about business as usual.'

'Carefully.'

'Yes. Just appear to be getting on with normal life stuff.'

'The police are coming back for a second interview today.'

'Don't tell them about the break in here.'

'You sure?'

'Yes.'

He nodded but I could see his reluctance. He was rattled. I didn't blame him.

My phone rang and I answered it immediately without looking at the number. 'Mum?'

'No darling, it's Liv. I have Cassandra with me.'

I let out a loud sigh of relief. 'Thank goodness. Is she OK?'

'Yes. But you should come now and get her.'

'On my way,' I said.

I hung up and pecked Garth on the cheek before leaping out of his car. 'Stay cool. I'll be in touch,' I said through the window.

Cass was okay. Suddenly the day felt better.

Ten minutes later I was striding along the long, disinfectant-heavy corridors at Charlies.

Liv was sitting up in bed in silk pyjamas fiddling with her manicure kit. Cass was staring out of the window, shoulders hunched. When Liv saw me she set the little plastic bag down on her food tray. 'Tara. How lovely. But you just caught me about to shower. Do you mind waiting?'

'Sure, Liv.'

She winked as she scooped her dressing gown up from the back of the chair and disappeared into the bathroom of her private room.

Cass didn't turn around or acknowledge my existence. Her normally cinnamon speckled aura was a molten mess.

'Cass, what's going on?'

She continued to ignore me, so I walked over to the window and stood beside her. We both stared out at the cars meandering around the car park.

'What did you hear?' I asked.

She shrugged at that. 'Don't matter.'

'Actually, it does. What you thought you heard and what was really going on in that conversation were two different things.'

She hunched further. 'I need to find somewhere to live.'

'No, you don't,' I said firmly. 'You're going to live with me.'

She stiffened at that. From the corner of my eye I could see her lower lip protruding stubbornly. I had to tread lightly.

'Don't you want to live in the new place too? You can decorate your room the way you like,' I asked.

She folded her arms. 'You want me to stay at your mum's.'

'I don't want you to stay there. I thought it was more responsible of me to have you stay there. In case you hadn't noticed, my lifestyle isn't exactly safe or ... regular.'

'Your mum didn't want me anyway.'

'My mother thinks you're wonderful. But she's using you to make me be more responsible. She hates what I'm doing with my life. She wants me married and holding white linen dinner parties.'

Cass didn't reply right away and I gave her a moment to let that process.

Finally, I added softly, 'I love Joanna, but our relationship is difficult. Always has been. I don't want you caught in the middle of it. And I don't want you at risk from my career choices.'

Cass turned to me, fists clenched. '*At risk?* Mum's an addict. My sister's an addict. My last boyfriend pimped for his mum after school. I had my teeth knocked out when I was twelve by one of my mother's *boyfriends*.' She used her fingers to draw imaginary quotes in the air around the latter. 'I've never felt—*been*—*safer* than when I'm with *you*!' She almost shouted the last word at me. Her aura slammed me. Tears filled her eyes but she kept them in check with anger.

My mouth fell open in surprise, and shame washed over me. How much had I really learned about her in the weeks she'd been living with me? I was always wrapped up in a case or my own ridiculous love life.

And yet, this was not a time to show Cass weakness. Like any teenager, she knew how to manipulate guilt.

'Hey,' I said. 'Let's make a deal.'

'What deal?' she asked continuing to glare with me.

'You live with me, but on the condition that you agree to do as I say, if I think a situation's not appropriate or safe for you.'

'Like what?'

'Like anything,' I said firmly. 'My rules.'

Her eyes narrowed while she considered my proposition. 'Can I set up an office for the business downstairs?'

'Yes. But you can only work in it when you're not at class or working the deli.'

'I don't work at the deli anymore.'

'Yes, you do,' I said. 'Joanna … sorted things.'

'But I don't *want* to work there.'

'You need the money.' *And the discipline*, I thought. But I didn't say it. I couldn't really; look at me. 'You work there until you finish your office diploma. Then we'll see.'

She picked at the cuticle of a fingernail. 'Fine.'

'Cass?'

She lifted her head. The tears were gone and her jaw had softened. 'I agree to the terms.' Then as an afterthought she added, 'Thanks.'

I nodded. 'Now let me drop you at the deli. See what shifts they have for you. Then I need to do some things. We'll clean it up and move in later today and tomorrow. But if you have time tonight, you can start packing gear into the boxes I left on the couch.'

She sprang up, suddenly energised. 'Let's go.'

'Hang on! I need to speak to Liv.'

The bathroom door opened on cue. 'Hot showers are a certain kind of bliss,' she said as she tucked her pyjamas and wet-pack in the narrow cupboard by the bed. She straightened up, and I saw she was wearing a loose dress and some sandals.

'Are they letting you go home today?'

'Yes, apparently. I'm just waiting to see the doctor.'

'We'll wait and give you a lift you,' I offered.

'No don't. It'll be a while yet. Joanna is coming with

Wallace.'

'Crap! I forgot to ring Mum!' I said remembering that she and Dad were still driving the streets of Euccy Grove searching for Cass.

I pulled at my phone and shot off a quick text. Then Cass and I kissed Liv goodbye in turns.

'I'll call in soon,' I said, adding in a hug for the woman who'd steered me through some of the worst periods of my life. 'Take it easy when you get home. No running around.'

'Goodness, you sound like Wallace. He's threatening to break out Monopoly to keep me still.'

'Sounds excruciating,' I said with a grin.

I glimpsed tiredness behind the bright smile she shone back at me. 'Actually, I don't mind.' She stared over my shoulder and out of the hospital window. 'I've been on my own a long time. It's rather sweet that someone wants to sit and play games with me.'

I squeezed her arm. 'He adores you.'

Her smile softened to affection. 'He's very caring and kind.'

I kept my expression mild, but I don't know that she and I were talking about the same guy. The Wal that I knew had an AK47 locked up in his wardrobe cum gun safe, and could take down a big, bad-guy biker in less than fifteen seconds.

But love was a funny thing.

'Bye,' I said.

And Cass and I headed out to the car park.

Cass didn't have much to say on the way back to the deli, and I didn't press her. We'd had one deep and meaningful today. For a teenager that was one too many.

She ducked into the deli while I waited and returned a short time later to tell me she had a daytime shift the next day.

'Right,' I said. 'Good. You can start packing.'

We caught all the green lights and were back at Lilac Street about seven minutes later.

Cass got out of the car while I checked my text messages. One from Tozzi. One from Ed. One from Garth.

I glanced up to tell Cass I'd catch up with her when I'd answered the three men in my life. She was halfway down the driveway and I saw a figure dressed in black detach from behind the three Cape Lilac trees between ours and the neighbour's fence. The figure had a hood pulled up over his head, despite the warm day and moved straight in close to Cass as if to touch her.

I flung myself out of the door and tried to run down the driveway in a flat-out sprint. My muscles still remembered how to do that from my days doing endless court runs, but my still-sore ankle complained like hell.

The figure had hold of Cass's hand and I didn't bother to shout. Instead I threw myself at him. It wasn't the first time I'd tackled someone. I knew what I was doing: head tucked, shoulder first, catch them around the knees.

The tall, lean figure went down like a felled sapling. Just kinda bent and buckled. I landed on his calves and felt the heels of his boots jab into my soft bits. Immediately, I rolled and got to my knees. I didn't have a weapon but there was a tree branch leaning against the house already neatly cut and ready to go into the birds' cage.

Dimly, I heard the birds screeching at the end of the driveway where the path led up to my flat. That wasn't good.

'Cass! Quick! Hand me that branch.'

She was standing there, hand over her mouth. Frozen.

'Casssss!' I yelled at her.

She jerked out of her trance and burst out laughing.

I glared up at her then down at the collapsed figure next to me, suddenly recognising leather guy, Bubba Pete.

He was holding his nose, which was bleeding, after having face-planted straight into the concrete floor.

The sight of it made me realise that my own knees were stinging from the impact. So were my wrists and palms. I thought, vaguely, that my cousin Crack would describe it as arm pump—the ache you got from gripping the handle bars of a motorbike over rough terrain.

'Sorry about that, Pete,' I said, offering a hand to pull him up.

He cast me a filthy look and got to his feet unassisted.

'Thith ith for you,' he said thickly, handing me a phone. 'Wanth you to ring thwaight away.'

173

Had I broken his nose? Please, Lord no! How would Bon Ames take me maiming his messenger boy?

'Cass, take Pete to the flat and clean him up. I'll just make this call.'

Cass held out a hand to the young biker who gave several backward glances to make sure I wasn't following too closely.

I trailed them slowly up the dip into the driveway, limping past the birds and into the garden. While they disappeared into the flat, I made myself familiar with Nightfire and Persephone again. Persephone's flowers were looking a little curled still.

The burner phone rang three times before my behemoth biker comrade answered.

'We've got a job for you,' he said.

'Hang on ... I thought we were ... you know ... settled.'

'Yeah. When we say so.'

I felt the knot return to my stomach. I didn't want this crap. I wanted Lindt white chocolate balls, and pepperoni pizza and easy jobs reading the body language of cheating married men. Bikies. Criminals. Too much! Dead bodies. Too much!

'What do you want?' Fear made me terse and short. Not that Bon Ames would notice blunt.

'Get close to the Kenilworth bitch.'

I felt a sudden rush of exasperation with Mr Cryptic and Scary. 'What? Just like that? I haven't spoken to her since school. I can't just waltz up and act like her best friend. And anyway, she probably doesn't know anything about anything. Sleaze balls like him never tell gorgeous women about their seedy activities.'

'If that's the case, she'll stay healthy.'

It was a statement. And I didn't feel good about the implication. Phoebe Kenilworth wasn't my kind of person, but I wasn't about to hand her over to the likes of the Western Cheaters.

'You need to give me a bit more,' I said. 'I got no idea what I'm looking for.'

He was silent for a few seconds.

'Let's just say that we provide certain products to sectors of the community. So did Romeo. It caused some problems between us.'

'You killed him?' I whispered.

'Sadly, no.'

'So?'

'Romeo should have kept information about his side business.'

'Can't you find that out for yourselves?'

Another pregnant pause.

'The people Romeo ran with. They're not our type. Jake thinks you'd be our best shot,' he said.

'Won't you find out in good time anyway?'

'That ain't the point.'

'You mean forewarned is forearmed,' I ventured.

'You need to get on this today. We're on a timeline,' he said.

They're on a timeline. Sheesh. For the thousandth time, I regretted my actions in Brisbane which had left me owing the Cheaters a favour. It had seemed a sensible decision in the moment. 'And if I find out where this information is, we'll be done?'

'Jake says, you do this for us, he's ready to consider an arrangement.'

'I don't want an arrangement.'

'People don't refuse Jake's arrangements,' said Bon. 'You got two days to find out what we need. Then I'll send Bubba around with a new burner.'

'I think I broke his nose.'

Yet another silence.

'Bon?'

'Fuck, Sharp,' he said, and hung up.

I tried uncurling one of Persephone's leaves to no avail. So I gave up and went to check on Pete and Cass. She had him leaning over the sink and was dabbing at his face.

'I don't think it's actually broke,' she said when she saw me.

I stayed at the door, not wanting to spook Pete who looked rather wild eyed. 'Good to hear. Sorry about that, but you shouldn't sneak up like that.'

He just kept staring at me, flashing the whites of his eyes.

'Right, well I have things to do. Don't stay long, my mother will be down to check on Cass.'

They both nodded, understanding my meaning. I pointed to the boxes. 'Cass, tape them up and then throw our stuff in. I'll be back later today.'

'What about Garth,' she said. 'You want to me to go there?'

'Who'th Garth?' said Pete.

'None of your beeswax,' I told him. And to Cass. 'No. Stay put.' I scooped up my laptop and headed out to Gloria Jeans. It was time for cake and uninterrupted WiFi.

Chapter 15

Call me shallow, but a date and honey loaf with butter and a large latte made me feel a whole lot better about the day.

I set up in a corner, kicked the spare chair over to another table and generally adopted a *don't bother me* hunch over my keyboard. Before I got down to research on Phoebe Kenilworth, I read my texts from Tozzi and Ed.

Tozzi's was inviting me to dinner tonight. Ed's was the same.

I looked at the ceiling and cursed Smitty. Then I rang her.

'Just a moment,' she puffed into the phone. Fridge has got Henry's … I'm just wrestling it … bad dog! Fridge! Oh! No … !'

I heard a crunch and then a slam.

'Bad time?' I asked.

She sighed heavily. 'I can't even blame this on you. He's

just chewed up Henry's stamp collection. Moth balls and all.'

'What was the dog doing with the stamp collection?'

'I was spring cleaning ...'

'Right. Well ... moral of the story you know.'

'Tell me something distracting.'

'Tozzi and Ed have both asked me out to dinner tonight. Who do I accept?'

'Ooh,' she said, in the tone she gets when a delicious morsel of gossip drops in her lap. 'Who do you want to accept?'

'If I knew that I wouldn't be ringing you,' I pointed out.

'What will you wear?'

'Hang on. I haven't even decided who I'm going with or if I'm even ...' I trailed off, hit with a sudden brainwave. I didn't have to accept either of them.

'T?' said Smitty suspiciously.

'I gotta go.'

'Fine, but you need to come to dinner. It's the only way you and Henny will get past the jaw thing.'

I sighed. 'Fine. Set it up for the weekend. Make sure Bok can come too.'

'More the merrier?'

'I was thinking more of *eat, drink and be merry* ...'

'Pessimist.'

'And it's served me well.'

I hung up and texted both of them back that I had a prior engagement. Then I started googling.

It turned out that Phoebe Kenilworth attracted the media almost as much as Nick's wife, Antonia. In fact, they were pictured online together at several social engagements. In one photo, they were even embracing and bestowing air kisses on each other. It shouldn't have been a surprise; they ran with the same set, yet seeing Antonia with her, settled a weight back on my chest.

I loved this city, but sometimes it felt like only half a degree of separation between me and everyone else.

Interestingly, there was nothing about her being the last person Bernard Romeo had seen before he died. Nothing about them knowing each other at all. Somehow, she'd managed to keep it all out of the public eye.

I made a list of people from school who knew both Phoebe and me. Then I crossed out the ones who would find it too weird to hear from me unexpectedly.

That left two names: Janis Hargrave and Sulia Yeo. Janis was a critical care nurse at Royal Perth Hospital and I couldn't imagine her having time or interest in socialite nonsense. Last I'd heard of Sulia she owned an expensive beauty salon upstairs in the Claremont Centre. That seemed more promising. Old school tie and all that crap.

I jotted down a few things I'd found out about Phoebe; that she'd been to Switzerland's last remaining finishing school, *Institut Villa Pierrefeu*, graduated from UWA in Business and Commerce with honours, and thanks to finding a list of current office bearers, she was on a Claremont Neighbourhood Watch committee, and—of course—a member of the Liberal Party.

I called Sulia's salon and made an appointment for a pedicure with 'their best person'. It must have been a slow morning, because they fitted me in straight away.

Melissa met me at the counter. She was an attractive woman with dark hair and a generous smile. She wore crisp clinic whites and her aura glowed pink with serenity. I liked her on sight.

She ushered me into a small room, lit the incense burner and checked that the meditation music was suitable.

It wasn't the first time I'd gone to a beauty salon for information. I hoped this time proved just as enlightening.

Once I was settled, Melissa sat on a stool and began the process of cleaning and preparing my feet. Some people can't bear pedicures. I adore them and listened blissfully as Melissa chatted. Later on, when she got to the calf massage, I made appropriately appreciative gargling noises.

At toe nail painting stage, I made my move. 'Melissa, that was wonderful,' I said. 'You were as good as they said you were.'

'Oh,' she said. 'May I ask who recommended me?'

'I can't remember,' I said vaguely. 'Might have been

Phoebe Kenilworth, I think.'

Melissa blushed and I felt a little guilty.

'That's kind of her,' she said.

'She does come here then? I got that right?'

'Oh, yes. Every Friday morning. She's one of our best clients.'

Friday was three days away. In two days I could be chopped up and fed to the fish in the Swan River.

'Oh, I should book in at the same time as her, so we can catch up,' I said, wracking my brains for another way to see Phoebe sooner.

Melissa's aura swirled a little faster, telling me that she was attempting to hold something in.

I gave her a little prompt. 'We go way back, you know. Went to school together,' I said and took another peek at her. 'That's how I know Sulia too.'

The mention of her boss slowed her aura down as if it was satisfied by my claims of connectedness. I waited, practising my most serene expression, and she finally ventured the information she'd been sweating over. 'Shame you didn't book in around lunchtime, Ms Kenilworth's coming in today as well.'

'Special occasion, no doubt?'

'Yes, so I believe. Tonight.'

'She's always had a busy social life being a Premier's daughter.'

Melissa nodded as she put the finishing strokes of top

coat on my toes. Her aura was in normal rhythm again and her lips pursed as she concentrated. She was too much of a professional to be drawn on anything more about another client, but what she'd told me was enough.

I paid up as soon as she let me go and promised I'd call for another appointment. Then I went across the street to the nearest coffee shop to wait until Phoebe came, so I could accidentally bump into her.

Knowing it would take a couple of hours, I ordered some food and sat eating, drawing up strategies in my mind to manage Garth's problem.

Someone clearly knew Garth was involved and potentially a danger to them. The messed-up office and the intruder in his home were soft approaches: a warning and an attempt to locate any incriminating evidence. They'd stop short of harming him physically, but that might change. I needed to come up with a strategy for him, or get him to hand it over to the police.

I spent the next hour reading everything I could find online about his new girlfriend and her partner. Grazia Santoro, Johnny Viaspa's sister had married into decent money on the face of things. Her boutique sold to high end middle-aged clients and tended towards tailored suits and eco-friendly dress clothes. The kind of place Liv would buy clothes. Maybe it was worth a call to her to see.

Grazia had two kids at private school according to her

Facebook page which was set to public. It was littered with recent family photos of two spoiled looking kids holidaying in the snow.

Grazia's husband was a portly, but handsome guy in his late forties with a classic dimpled chin. A hundred years ago and few kilos lighter he would have made a great black and white movie star. Grazia, herself, was glamorous in a heavily made up kind of way. Her hair wasn't lacquered to attention in the way that Eireen Tozzi's was, but a decade or two and I could it see happening.

I'd bet though, that Grazia didn't have anywhere near the chutzpah that Eireen possessed—the woman was the devil in tiny black pumps and chunky gold earrings. Grazia also had the misfortune of being part of the Viaspa bloodline.

It was harder to find information on Jasmine Kaflouti. She'd gone to Palmyra High School then completed a fashion certificate at TAFE. Aside from a lot of photos at social events, there wasn't a lot more to find. She knew enough about Facebook that her profile was set to private and her LinkedIn page showed nothing I hadn't already learned.

I glanced up from my online sleuthing and saw a taxi pull into the kerb in front of the salon. I recognised the woman who was leaning over the backseat to pay the cabbie, so I slapped some change down on the table and bolted across the street, timing my trajectory to intersect with Phoebe just as she emerged from the cab.

'I'm so sorry,' I gasped. 'I didn't—why goodness … Phoebe Kenilworth …'

She staggered backwards from the impact of our collision, but the annoyance on her face dissolved a little as she tried to work out who I was.

'Tara,' I said, obligingly. 'We went to school together.'

She frowned, drawing down hard on her memory. I noticed the dark rings under her eyes, and the blotches on her otherwise perfect skin that suggested she'd be crying recently. 'I'm sorry, I don't think that I—'

'You probably knew my cousin Crack better? Err … I … mean Craig Thorn.'

The coin dropped. 'Craig Thorn, yes. Oh, you're umm … Tara … umm … Sharp. You were the one caught with a boy in the sports shed?'

I couldn't help the blush. It was a long time since anyone had mentioned that particular indiscretion of mine. Infamy, huh. 'Rumours,' I said blithely. 'Just added to my mystique.'

'That's funny,' she said. 'I thought you got suspended.'

I laughed as a distraction. 'Do you go to this salon? I adore it. Melissa's my favourite.'

She smiled, realising that I was changing the subject, and was polite enough to let it go. 'Yes. Indeed. Anyway, speaking of … I'd best get moving. Things to do.'

'Yes, me too. Are you going to that big thing tonight?' I just threw it out there. People like Phoebe were always going to some "big" thing.'

'You mean the Hilton parade. Yes, I am, I'm afraid. No rest for the wicked.' She shook her head a little sadly. 'Nice seeing you again, Tara. Bye.'

She glided inside and I moved on until I was around the corner out of sight. Parade? What parade? I got out my phone and tried googling general terms, but was deluged with information. It wasn't until I got back to Mona that it hit me. She meant fashion parade.

I immediately texted Garth. Jasmine's fashion parade. When and where?

The reply came quickly. Tonight. Hilton ballroom.

That had to be it, I thought. It would give me a more natural and less obvious way to get chatting with her. I could also tail her afterwards. See what she did.

Garth sent a second text. ??????

I need two tickets. I replied.

Will ask Jasmine to leave them on the door.

Thanks.

Our exchange over, I doubled back towards my car. My phone rang and I answered it quickly, forgetting to look at the caller ID.

'Hey,' said Nick Tozzi.

'Hey,' I said, my heart beating faster.

'Did you get my text?'

'Sorry, I haven't read it yet. I've been busy. Two jobs running at once.'

'I won't ask,' he said.

'Don't. How are you after …?' I wanted to say *puking*, but I refrained, 'the run?'

'Sore. Embarrassed. Thanks for the wakeup call though. Didn't realise how out of shape I'd got.'

'It was unfair of me,' I said. 'I've been running that hill for a while.'

'Well, you're never one to make allowances, are you?' His voice was honey laden and I imagined his aura glimmering with the same golden glow. 'I rang to see if you'd come to a fashion parade with me tonight.'

'The one at the Hilton?'

'Yes, do you know about it?'

'I'm already going,' I said.

'Oh.'

He sounded so disappointed that I softened. 'We could still sit together if you like.'

'My tickets are front row,' he said.

No doubt Phoebe Kenilworth's were too. Tozzi would be a perfect cover for me. 'Sounds better than the back row. Why are you going to a fashion parade anyway?'

'I'm part of the charity contingent. They auction some of their front row tickets for ridiculous prices and give the proceeds to the Telethon Kids research.'

Nice,' I said. I hadn't thought about Tozzi as a

philanthropist.

'Sh-shall I pick you up?' He was as hesitant as a teenager asking a girl out on a first date and any resistance I had melted away.

'Sure … oh, actually. You'd better come and get me from my new place.'

There was silence on the other end for a moment. 'Which would be …?'

'The Gar Lok.'

'Of course it is. Who else would live in a Chinese restaurant?'

It was hard to tell if he was being funny or not. 'Recently closed down Chinese restaurant,' I corrected him.

'See you at seven.'

I called Smitty immediately. 'Get a sitter. I need you to come to a fashion parade at the Hilton with me tonight.'

'Oh but—'

'No buts Jane Smith. Tozzi's taking me and I have to work. You're going to keep him out of my hair for a while. You owe me.'

'How do you figure,' she said with an edge of amusement in her voice.

'You told me to tell him to slow down, and now he's trying to date me.' I could hear the slight tone of hysteria rising in my voice.

Smitty laughed. 'I haven't been out in ages. It sounds fun. When and where.'

'Meet me at the Gar Lok at 6.45PM.'

'Oh goodness,' she said. 'I can hardly wait.'

I pointed Mona towards Lilac Street and returned to find Cass surrounded by boxes. I threw some masking tape at her and together we taped up all our belongings.

When we were done, we took a run to the new place with a bag of cleaning gear and JoBob's vacuum cleaner. I set Cass to work picking up all the large items of rubbish, while I drove the vac. When we'd finished, Cass had three large Tidy bags full. We then split the kitchen and the bathroom between us. I scrubbed the grout in the tiles while Cass wiped benches and swept out cupboards.

A couple of hours later, we were back at Lilac Street lugging our belongings out to the car. My belongings, I should say. Hers amounted to one small box, the weight of which was largely made up of the cookbooks Joanna had loaned her. As soon as I had some cash flow, I was going to have to get her some clothes.

'We'll have to make a couple of trips,' I said. 'I'll go and hook the trailer up.'

She didn't seem bothered with the idea of more work. The excitement of moving had taken over everything. 'Your mum came down to see me earlier.'

'How was that?'

'Awkward,' she said. 'Huggy.'

I bit my lip. Huggy with Joanna was most definitely awkward.

'She said that you could take anything you want from the storage shed, and that she and your dad were going up to the Hills today to visit her sister-in-law.'

I nodded. They did that about once a month. Dutifully. Without exception. 'Right then. Let's get on with it!'

By dinner time we had everything moved, including some other things I'd grabbed from storage: crockery, pots, and cutlery from my last sojourn on my own, a small chest of drawers, three kitchen chairs and a square kitchen table JoBob had discarded years ago. The couch was the last thing we tied onto the trailer. Fortunately, it was cane and not too heavy, and my bed had pulled apart. The mattresses proved the heaviest, but by then we were on a high, and on a roll.

When it was all deposited at the other end, we guzzled down some ginger ale and flopped on the carpet in the main room next to each other.

'I can still smell sweet and sour sauce,' I said.

'And garlic,' Cass added. 'The kitchen is awesome.'

She was right. Possibly, it was the best feature of the whole place, outside the light shades and statue of Buddha in this room. 'This will be good too, when we can afford some furniture.'

She nodded. 'Yeah the air con works a treat. And there's lots of light.'

'I'm going to a fashion parade tonight,' I said.

'This to do with Garth or the Cheaters?'

'Well Garth will be there. His girlfriend's boutique is supplying some of the clothes. But yeah, it's for Bon Ames.'

'I'd like to meet him,' she said.

'I'd like for that not to happen.'

'He was famous around my old neighbourhood, y'know. The boys—my mates—all crushed on him.'

'Funny kind of crush,' I observed.

She shrugged. 'Sergeant of Arms carries heaps of respect in Bunka.'

'Yeah well, once I do this job for them, they're out of my life. And I don't want them ever to be in yours.'

She rolled away from me, as if annoyed. I wondered if Pete was the cause of it.

'I'd better get showered and changed. Tozzi's picking Smitty and me up,' I said. I wasn't about to let Cass's sulks bother me. My house. My rules. *Stand firm*, I told myself.

She rolled back over, her interest piqued. 'Three of you going together?'

I grinned at her. 'Safety in numbers.'

By the time I'd showered and unearthed my dressing gown from the chaos of my suitcases, I realised I was starving, and went in search of Cass.

She was downstairs in the kitchen, arranging the odds and ends we'd brought from Lilac Street. Our few kitchen items looked pitifully miniscule in the restaurant grade kitchen, but Cass didn't seem to notice. She was carefully separating out the cutlery and plates and allotting them spaces.

'We forgot to raid Joanna's kitchen,' I said mournfully, spying the tools but no the food.

'She sent some stuff,' said Cass.

'What do you mean?' I hadn't seen Joanna since this morning's conversation.

She gestured to an esky over near the fridge that I hadn't noticed before.

'Where did that come from?'

'Wal brought it. She must have phoned him.'

'Wal?'

'Here,' called a voice from the front room.

I pushed open the swinging door and peered in. Wal was on the floor under the counter. He rolled to his feet in a single movement and held up a power board. 'I've vacuumed. Now I'm just sorting the outlets before the desks arrive.'

'What desks?' Why did I feel I was the last to know everything?

A knocking at the door was all the answer I got, as Wal hustled across to open it.

It was Smitty, dressed in a slimline, pink crepe dress

with lace in all the right places. She looked sweet and beautiful all wrapped into one and her killer pink heels lent some height and elegance. She had her hair pulled back, subtle make-up on, and was carrying a large bag.

Wal swayed under the force of her femininity, and almost swept a bow as she walked past him.

'You look ...'

'Awesome,' Cass finished for me, poking her head out of the kitchen.

I nodded. 'Truly Smitts, you do.'

She smiled, delighted. 'Nice to know I've still got a bit of something left.'

'More than a bit, I'd say.'

She looked me up and down. 'Thank goodness I came early. Lead on to the bedroom MacDuff. Time to get you glammed up too.'

I showed her upstairs to my room and she immediately spotted the dress trousers and shirt I had out ready to wear.

'I suspected as much,' she cried waving the bag in her hand. 'Bok sent this for you to wear.'

Bok and Smitty had spent years trying to mould my fashion sense, one taking over when the other gave up for a while. But Bok only ever sent me sample dresses when I had something special on.

'How did you ...'

'I went straight over to the office to see him after you

rang. He called in a favour. You have to return it though.'

'What is it?' I asked, staring at the bag with suspicion.

'Proenza Schuler. It's straight from the spring collection in New York and totally divine.'

'Never heard of her.'

Smitts tapped me lightly on the cheek. 'Don't show your ignorance, T. Get the damn thing on.'

I retrieved the dress from the bag as though I was pulling a trick scarf from a top hat.

When I finally held it in front of me, my heart beat faster. It was an aqua blue, sleeveless dress that had a tunic top which finished in a fringed skirt. The fringes started just below my panty line. A 1920s style with a twist.

My eyes popped a little. 'Jeez.'

'I'm going downstairs to stall Tozzi. Get it on and leave your hair out. Pink lipstick. Blue sandals I gave you two years ago. Are your legs shaved?'

I nodded dumbly. 'I can't go out—'

'Oh, for goodness sakes. It's THE parade of the year. You can go naked if you like.'

Well I certainly wasn't planning on that.

She left me with the dress, which I turned over in my hands. Whichever way you looked at it the fringe skirt was risqué.

I took a deep breath. My friends never steered me wrong. Have faith.

I slipped it on and managed the zip alone. Then I pulled

my hair free of its tie and ran a brush through. It took me a bit longer to find the sandals in the boxes, but finally I was assembled. Halfway out the door, I remembered the pink lipstick and returned to hunt for it in my old school pencil case.

I heard more knocking as I descended the stairs carefully. I hadn't been in true high heels for a while and felt a bit wobbly. Fortunately, I had no mirror in the bedroom yet, so I was spared the trauma of my own critical gaze.

As I entered the room, I saw Nick looking admiringly at Jane. 'Good to see you again Jane. How's Hen—'

He broke off when he saw me, his jaw sagging open. His aura deepened from its normal caramel to something almost chocolatey.

Smitty and Wal turned to look at me and Wal's face flushed a shade of beetroot. Wal's aura ran to smoky grey most of the time, but right now it was almost black. Smitty's looked normal and her expression was smug.

'H-hi!' I stammered, feeling self-conscious. In my heels, I topped about six feet four inches, and no doubt the fringe was making that seem like most of it was my legs.

Nick kept on staring, while Wal's eyes shot to the ceiling and back, like he was checking I was real.

'Jeez,' I said. 'What's wrong with you two? It's just a dress.'

Tozzi managed to shut his mouth and regain some

composure. 'That might be a tiny bit of an understatement, Tara,' he said. 'You look …'

'You look like you need to put on a coat,' Wal finished for him in a mildly outraged, fatherly kind of way.

I shook my head in disgust at them both and glanced at Cass who was peering around the kitchen door.

'Cool,' said Cass, giving me the thumbs up. It was her single word approval that bolstered my confidence. If she'd curled her lip, I might have run back upstairs to hide under my bed. Instead, I picked up my Mandarina Duck, and linked my arm through Jane's.

'Let's go,' I said.

Chapter 16

The Hilton lobby thronged with beautifully dressed people gliding about. As we caught the crowded lift to the ballroom, I decided most of them were going to the parade as well.

Nick shadowed Smitts and me, and as we emerged from the lift he took my arm in a purposeful manner. It was a togetherness statement that, combined with my swinging fringe skirt, made me as uncomfortable as hell.

'Our seats are there,' he said pointing to the centre of the front row.

'Goodness,' I said. 'Who'd you murder for those?'

He grimaced. 'My wallet. It's still bleeding.'

'Well they look wonderful, but there's only two. I should sit with Smitts in the seats that I was given,' I said.

Tozzi's expression became mildly thunderous and his aura prickled against me.

'No way,' piped up Smitts from down near Tozzi's elbow. 'I'm the gooseberry tonight. I was expecting back stalls and that's exactly what I want: a place to chill out and not have to speak to anyone.'

Before I could argue, she'd dashed over to the door and secured the free tickets Garth had arranged. Waving cheerily, she disappeared off across the ballroom to row Z.

'Why do I get the feeling you're embarrassed to be seen with me,' said Nick grumpily.

'Don't be ridiculous,' I said. 'Let's sit. People are looking at my legs.'

His frown vanished in favour of a slightly lecherous smile. 'Indeed.'

He went first, but kept hold of my hand, drawing the attention of too many people. For a start, everyone knew Nick Tozzi, and no doubt his wife Antonia. And then for those who didn't, we were simply the tallest people in the room. Then there was the small matter of the amount of flesh I was showing.

Despite the air conditioning, I was breaking a sweat by the time we reached our seats. Once seated though, I began to relax. The music was good and we were no longer being ogled by two hundred plus people. Maybe this would be fine, even possibly pleasant, I told myself.

'You OK?' asked Tozzi, leaning close to my ear.

I felt his aura softening against me and his breath on my shoulder. The combination was far too titillating, so I tried to think about other things. Like the reason I was here. Phoebe Kenilworth.

'I shouldn't have worn this dress,' I said.

'You absolutely should have,' he said.

'I'm not sure how to take that,' I said.

'I'll explain, in detail, later.'

I would have pressed him on it, but I spied Phoebe sitting at the end of the front row on the opposite side. She got up, put her brochure down and headed towards the sign that read Restrooms.

Perfect! 'I'll be back in a moment. Just seen someone I need to speak to.'

'It'll be starting in just under ten minutes,' he said looking at his watch. 'They don't like it if you're not seated by then.'

'Back in a flash,' I said.

'Tara?'

'Promise!'

He grunted and turned to the woman next to him who was tapping on his arm. Tozzi was never short of people wanting to talk to him.

I escaped through to the back rows and circumnavigated the room. From my lofty six feet four inch vantage point, I spied Smitty directly opposite Nick and me across the catwalk, but in the last row. She was chatting to the woman next to her and happily sipping her complimentary champagne.

Further perusal of the venue revealed Bok off-stage but near where the models would enter. He was talking with a person who, I guessed, from his interesting garb, was a designer. I felt a wave of reassurance. Smitty and Bok were both here.

Smiling to myself, I turned away to follow Phoebe into the restroom and bumped straight into a couple who'd just entered through the main doors. The man righted me with a hand on my arm.

'Pardon me, I'm so—' I started to say and then broke off.

Jake Stranger was my collision partner, and tottering next to him on heels that would have made my nose bleed, was his sulky girlfriend.

'Jeez,' I breathed. 'What the hell are you doing here?'

Jake glanced around to assess who could hear us, and then shot me an appraising look. 'Wow.'

His girlfriend's expression turned from sulky to malevolent, and I had an awful flash of her pulling a pistol from her clutch and shooting me.

Don't be ridiculous, I told myself, after a peep at her purse. *It's much too small to fit a revolver.*

'I mean, if you're here, why am I?' I said.

The admiration bled out of his features. I could see the tattoo peeping up over his collar and his hand on my arm tightened. 'Just do what you came here to do.'

We locked gazes and after a moment I nodded and pulled my arm from his grip.

I cast a quick look over my shoulder, to see if anyone

had noticed our encounter. From the sea of faces, and the blur of auras, one stood out. John Viaspa. He was staring straight at us from the second row, down near the foot of the runway. Why hadn't I seen him before? What in the hell was he doing here?

I thought for a second that I might throw up: Jake Stranger and now *Viaspa*—a big ol' black hole of bad karma in one room that totally cancelled out the comfort I felt from Smitts and Bok being there.

I hadn't seen Viaspa since Brisbane. Before I went there, he'd put a contract out on me, but since the person he'd hired had been arrested by the police, he'd decided to lay low. I assumed that was because he was trying to distance himself from hiring someone to kill me. Then in Brisbane, Bon Ames had come to my rescue. That was why I was in this predicament with them, why I owed them.

I turned and headed to the restroom. When I was safely inside, I leaned against the wall and tried to steady my breathing.

Phoebe Kenilworth was at the basin applying lippy. She glanced up and saw me.

'Oh, hello.' Her eyebrows lifted. 'Goodness. You should be on the catwalk in that outfit, Tara. You look …'

'Phoebe. Hi! But please hold that thought,' I said interrupting her. 'I wish I'd never worn the damn thing.'

She smiled, but her face looked pale and pinched. She put her lipstick away into her tiny white-ribboned clutch.

'Well, just between you and me, I'd rather be anywhere but here too,' she sighed.

I rallied from my double shot of Jake Stranger/Johnny Viaspa shock and went over to the basin. 'I guess you get sick of these things?'

She shook her head. 'It's not that. It's just that I … well …,' she lowered her voice. 'I don't mean to get too personal … but I … lost someone close to me recently … I'm still in—'

She broke off as a toilet flushed and someone exited one of the stalls and joined us at the basins. I took my comb out and ran it through my hair, while Phoebe touched up her concealer.

The woman dried her hands under the blower and left, and I dived into the opening Phoebe'd given me. 'Yes, it changes your perspective about these kinds of things, doesn't it?' I said gently. Her cool blue aura, which had been throbbing, began to flake: slender shreds of cobalt floating off into the air around us both. She was a mess and I wanted to give her a hug.

'Yes, he was. And his … death … was … horrible …' she shuddered.

I leaned over and patted her back—near her heart— just where the worst of the flakes were peeling off, and tried to stem the flow. 'You don't mean Bernard Romeo, by any chance, do you?'

She flinched and glanced at me with fear in her eyes.

'How do you know?'

I pressed gently on the same spot, still trying to stem the flaking. 'Nothing. It's just that his death was in the papers recently, and I took a guess. I do this kind of thing for a living. Two and two, I mean.'

My answer seemed to calm her a little. 'Please don't mention this to anyone. Our ... relationship wasn't ... well, not many people knew about it. I don't want the press hounding me. And ...' she flushed, 'he was married.'

'No judgement from me,' I said softly. 'I have enough problems with my own love life.'

She managed a small smile. 'Was that Nick Tozzi, you walked in with?'

'Oh, you saw us?'

'A little hard not to. From one school chum to another ... you want to watch that wife of his. She's a loose cannon.'

I nodded. 'Thanks. I know. Hey, if you ever want a friendly ear, I've just moved into the old Gar Lok restaurant. That is, I'm living upstairs.' I fished a business card out of my bag. 'And—'

Someone else entered the toilet, and I stopped.

She pursed her lips and nodded. 'Thanks, Tara. Take care.'

I waited a few moments, before I followed her out, knowing that I'd cracked the ice, established a connection. But it wasn't enough. I hadn't learned enough.

I thought about moving interstate again. Phoebe was a

nice woman, a sad woman. I didn't want to embroil her in anything to do with Jake Stranger.

As I wrenched open the door, the music shifted gears and the lights dimmed. I couldn't see Stranger, or Viaspa which was something. I hustled back to my seat, as quickly as my heels would let me, and plopped down next to Tozzi as the compère began introducing the designer lines.

'Cut that fine,' he breathed.

His huge hand engulfed mine, and I sensed the women around us exchanging glances.

I slipped my hand out of his grip and folded my arms. I'd never given any thought to what dating Nick Tozzi might be like, and I suddenly didn't feel ready for this kind of scrutiny.

'What is it?' he whispered to me as the first models appeared and began to sashay down.

'Everyone's staring at us,' I said.

'Ignore them,' he said.

'Easy for you to say. You're not the one with a fringe up to your breakfast.'

His hand moved to my knee and began to slide along my leg. 'Thanks for reminding me.'

'Jeez,' I said and clamped my knees together.

He sighed in a resigned kind of way and removed his wandering fingers. 'Honestly, you'll get used to it. It means nothing.'

'No,' I said sinking lower in my seat. This whole

arriving-with-Tozzi-plus-fringe-dress had been one of the worst ideas I'd had in a long time. 'I doubt it.'

The models were coming in waves now, jutting their hips out in unnatural poses, turning their angular jaws, and dishing out bland expressions.

I'd been to a bunch of similar shows over the years, usually for fundraisers, and usually under protest. But for the first time, it really struck me how I truly abhorred the whole concept of them. Not so much the exhibition of the clothes, but more the ridiculous standards the models were held to, and the focus on physical beauty. Yet, here I was in a butt-revealing dress, all in the name of fashion. The size of the scowl on my face matched my disgust in myself.

Tozzi could see it too. 'Can't you pretend to enjoy it,' he whispered.

'It's a bloody meat market,' I said.

To my surprise, he agreed with me. 'Yes, but it means fifteen thousand dollars to the new children's hospital. And it's a creative art. We need to support those kinds of things. So keep it in perspective.'

I glanced at him. I think I'd just learned something new about my date. *Silver linings.*

The music ramped up as the first part of the show reached its crescendo, and I slipped my hand across and gave his a squeeze. 'You're really a good guy, you know that.'

He grinned but didn't turn his head. 'That's what I've been trying to tell you.'

I was busy smiling at him when something happened. A cooing noise from the largely female crowd drew my attention back to the runway. A male model had emerged and was standing there in an open shirt which showed off his immaculate pecs, a pair of Hugo Boss knit trousers, a bow tie, and a set of angels wings pinned to his back.

Spontaneous applause broke out. It was Ed, looking chiselled and divinely divine.

My mouth dropped open. Firstly, it hadn't occurred to me that he might be working this gig. Secondly, I mean, I knew he was gorgeous, but seeing him up there, in his element, strutting his stuff was something else. The theme song from the *Magic Mike* movies started up, and most of the female audience got to their feet and started clapping.

'Isn't that your … friend?' said Tozzi, his expression tightening.

I swallowed. 'Umm … that's Ed, yeah.'

Ed began to move down the runway, half dancing, half-strutting, with an elegance that made Channing Tatum seem clumsy.

Every few steps he stopped and connected with the audience, smiling, gyrating, and dancing: titillating the women closest to him, and many of the men too, I guessed.

In about thirty seconds, he was going to be in front of me. I hadn't known he was working on this parade, and he hadn't known I was coming. It shouldn't be an awkward moment, but it was going to be. Especially when he saw Nick Tozzi at my side. I let go of Tozzi's elbow. How was I going to explain this? Where was Jane? Where was Bok? Help! I needed a distraction.

The good Lord answered my prayers in a wicked way.

'Nicholas! What is *she* doing in my seat?' In the lull between music tracks changing, Antonia Tozzi's voice was like a razor blade scraping glass: loud, scratchy, and shiver inducing.

She stood in front of us in a stunning white dress that left her flawless, tanned midriff bare. Her hair was upswept and immaculate, with just two golden tendrils spiralling around her face. Save for the look of petulant fury on her face, she smelled and looked like the Madonna of haute couture.

The music kicked in again and I trembled under the clamber of competing sights and sounds: Ed's moment of recognition and confusion before the music carried him onward; Toni Tozzi's blazing aura that shot mortars of energy in my direction; and the heat radiating from Nick, as he looked up at his estranged wife.

'Toni, go and sit somewhere else. You're making an unnecessary scene.'

'Unnecessary!' she shrieked above the sound. 'You've given your slut my front row seat!'

Slut! I felt my own body heat ignite, and I stood up.

Just a few seats away from me, Jake Stranger watched with interest and his lady friend's smug, narrow-eyed expression nauseated me. Viaspa would be watching too, but I avoided looking for him.

The music started again and Ed danced past again on his way back down the catwalk, trying to maintain his indifference to the ugly little scene developing in the middle of his big moment.

I glanced around desperately for Smitty or Bok, and instead of them, I caught sight of Phoebe Kenilworth heading towards the door.

'Gotta run,' I told Nick curtly, and before Toni Tozzi could embarrass all of us any further, I bailed.

'Tara,' he lurched after me, but Toni latched onto his arm like someone falling off a cliff, and together they sank down into the seats.

I kicked Jake Stranger's outstretched foot as I hustled past, and caught a glimpse of Johnny Viaspa getting up to follow me. As soon as I was out of the ballroom, I shucked off my sandals, sprinted down the stairs and out onto the pavement.

It was dark now, but I caught sight of Phoebe in the street lights, walking down towards the river, and I hurried down the hill after her. She looked like she was going to the park in front of the river, but at the last moment she turned into a street and walked towards some flats. When she reached the brick letterbox outside she looked about then went down into a driveway undercroft.

I glanced over my shoulder. No Viaspa, so I slowed my pace and approached from the other side of the road, using the parked cars as cover. When I reached the post box opposite, I crouched behind it and peered around.

Phoebe had her back to me and was talking to a short, round man in a flamboyant Hawaiian shirt. Something about him was familiar. I was sure I knew him from somewhere.

He had his hand on her elbow but she shook it off. The hand moved to her hip. And then he groped her butt.

She pushed him back, repulsed. I crept across the street to take photos of them, but the light was low and the flash went off.

'What was that?' said the guy.

They turned in my direction, so I ran a few steps along the street, stepped over a low hedge in front of a renovated cottage and crouched down behind it. Moments later Phoebe's heels clicked past me on the pavement. I pressed against the hedge, my fringe-exposed butt scraping the scratchy grass.

Then something bit me. Lots of something. Hot pokers of pain attacked my bum and thighs. *Fricking green ants.*

As soon as she'd gone far enough past, I leapt up and over the hedge, feeling under the dress to locate the bities.

That's where Nick Tozzi found me, dancing about, shoes off, and with my hand up my fringed skirt.

'What are you doing, Tara?'

'Owwww!' I yowled glaring at him. 'Go away.'

'I came to apologise for my wi—'

'Eeeehh.' Another wave of hot-poker-pain swept my nether regions. 'Get them off!'

'Get what off?'

'Owwww! S-s-stupid fringe. F-frigging g-green ants in my pants!'

He went into immediate action mode, pulling off his jacket and holding it up in front of me to shield me from the headlights of cars driving along the road. Of course that did nothing to protect me from the cottage and nearby apartment windows, but I was beyond caring.

'Quick. Strip your underwear off. I'll shield you,' he said.

I went to work as he suggested and ripped my knickers down. In the glow of the streetlights, I saw the offending ants writhing about inside them, so I turned my underwear inside out and shook it. Satisfied the bities were gone I quickly slipped it back on. The pain was getting worse though. I needed ice.

'Can you go get the car? The pain ... I don't think I can walk.'

'On my way,' he said. 'What about Jane though?'

'I'll text her. But please hurry,' I said. 'I need to get into a cold shower or something.'

He loped off up the street, leaving me to let Smitts

know. I crouched down and laboured over the text.

Work stuff took me outside. Stung by green ants. ALL OVER!!!!! Going home. Grab taxi and I'll pay.

When I was done, I screwed up my eyes again, willing the pain away. Green ant bites could sting for a few minutes or hours depending on the species and the amount of venom they injected. I'd once squashed one with my big toe and had been in agony for almost a day.

This was multiple bites on a tender part of my anatomy. I needed cool water and ice packs. And some privacy.

Tozzi was back in record time, but it still felt like hours. Tears streamed down my face as he opened the car door for me, and all I wanted to do was swear.

'Home,' I managed to grind out.

He grimaced in sympathy and reached into the back seat, producing a silver ice bucket full of ice cubes.

'Help yourself,' he said. 'I promise not to peek.'

'You hero!' I gasped.

My phone made a series of buzzing sounds: texts coming in from Jane, Bok and Ed. I couldn't deal with any of them.

'Eyes on the road,' I told Tozzi. And with an almost choking relief, I clamped ice cubes onto my crotch.

Chapter 17

I told Nick to go home when we arrived at the Gar Lok.

'Don't be stupid about this, Tara. People can suffer anaphylactic shock from green ant bites,' he said as I got out of the car.

'It would have happened already,' I replied. 'I just need to lie down for a bit. And next time you ask a girl on a date, make sure it's not to sit in your ex-wife's seat.'

'I'm sorry. I had no idea. We're not together. She's just trying to make it … hard for me.'

'Well now's not the time to hash it out. I'm sorry you missed the second half of the show.' I wasn't really, but my upbringing dictated that I finished up politely.

He managed a smile. 'Never a dull moment …'

'Backatcha,' I said with meaning and shut the car door.

I went straight to bed with the rest of the ice, and slowly the pain began to ebb. The ignominy of my experience grew though. I'd taken my undies off in the middle of an—albeit dark—street. Thank goodness there'd been no one much around to see.

I picked up my phone and studied the snap of Phoebe and the short, round man. I was sure of it. But from where …?

Maybe if I occupied my mind with something else it would come back to me, so I checked my texts and replied to Smitts telling her that I was AOK and at home with my friend, Mr Ice Cube.

My reply to Ed was harder.

His text had simply read

?????

Finally I settled for

Let's meet for coffee tomorrow afternoon if you can. I'll explain. X

'Tara,' said Cass.

I looked up at the doorway. 'Hey.'

'There's someone downstairs to see you. She says her name is Phoebe.'

'Here?'

Cass nodded. 'I left her in the office. You going to come down?'

I scrambled up out of bed and checked the time on my phone. 10.30PM. 'Yes. Get her drink and tell her I'll be there in a minute.'

Cass nodded. She hadn't even laughed at me when I'd come limping in. She was a good kid.

I slipped into loose shorts and a t-shirt, pulled my hair

into a pony tail and went bare feet down to see Phoebe. You call in on a girl late at night, you get what you get.

I found her sitting stiffly on the couch holding a glass of water. She hadn't changed from the parade. Cass was leaning awkwardly on the counter, and looked thankful to see me.

Soon as I appeared, she vamoosed back into the kitchen.

Phoebe watched her go and then looked sadly at me.

'Phoebe?' I went to sit next to her on the couch. 'What's wrong?'

'Sorry to call in so late, Tara. I got home and looked you up online. I see you really are an investigator.'

'Of a sort,' I said cautiously. 'We just moved in today. You'll have to excuse the mess.'

She nodded absently.

'What can I do for you,' I added.

'I'd like to hire you. I assume you have client confidentiality contracts or NDAs?'

Nondisclosure agreements weren't something I'd had to deal with so far. 'I can have Cass send you an agreement as soon as we're settled in here. But firstly, we need to talk a little.'

'You do private detective work?' she said, seeking assurance.

'I do specialised jobs. I'm not licensed.'

'Oh?'

'I do some investigation, but my role is more advisory. I have a talent for reading people. What is it you'd be wanting from me?'

She sipped some water and put the glass down on the upturned box that Cass had dragged close to her to use as a side table.

'Can I trust you, Tara?' she whispered.

'Absolute trust and discretion for my clients. Yes.'

'I think that my ... Bernard was involved in some ... well ... criminal activity.'

'What do you mean?'

She licked her lips and folded her hands in her lap as if determined to get something off her chest. 'We'd been seeing each other for about six months. It was very ... intense. He was always so attentive. Charming. The dearest man.'

'But?'

'I don't know really. He drowned, you know. Washed up on a South Cottesloe beach. I mean ... he shouldn't have been swimming then. We had a date earlier that night. He'd left me and gone home.'

'Home to his wife?'

'Yes?' Her gaze dropped.

'Have you spoken to the police?' I asked.

'Yes. They aren't the problem. Bernard disappeared after he left my place.'

'What's the problem then?'

'Someone ... an a-associate of Bernard's keeps following me. Insisting I have something of Bernard's that he wants.'

'Scaring you?'

'Yes.'

'You should talk to the police about it.'

'No! If Bernard was involved in something ... awkward, his name will be dragged through the mud. His family will be. It's bad enough that he and I were ...'

'Do they know?'

She shook her head. 'We were careful.'

I bit my lip. You can't be careful enough in Perth.

'And then there's my father ... if there's even a hint that I'm connected with anything dubious, they'll crucify my family.'

'Your father must have people who can handle this kind of thing?'

'I don't want him involved at all. This is my life. I want to hire you to find who this man is, so I can make him go away. I don't want anything to taint Bernie's funeral. Please Tara. Help me!'

I thought about my position. The Cheaters wanted me to get close to Phoebe and ask questions. Now that I was in a position to do that, it was the last thing I wanted to do. I liked Phoebe. She was mourning for Bernard. I didn't want her dragged into anything. But maybe, now, I had the opportunity to protect her.

'What does the guy think you have?'

She shrugged and looked at me with such weariness, I thought she might just curl up on the couch and pass out. 'Are you going to help me? I mean … I should have said earlier … I can pay whatever your rates are.'

'Yes. I will help.'

A little tremble of relief moved through her.

'Do you know this man's name? Have a picture of him?'

'No picture. He turned up at my door the morning after Bernie drowned. He's been following me ever since. Even tonight, after the parade. I'm s-scared he might do something to me. He seems desperate. Unpredictable.'

My mind spun with possibilities and I watched her aura for clues. It was turbulent but not as flaky as before.

'Listen, I'm going to send a guy to watch you. His name is Wallace—Wal. He'll keep you safe from this man while I do some background checks. When I know what we're dealing with I'll be in touch. OK?'

She seized my hands in hers and laid her face over them. 'Thank you,' she whispered. 'What do you need?'

'The names and contact numbers for any of Bernard's friends that you've met. Also, do you know if he kept a safe at home?'

'I'm not sure that I can be of much help there. We kept separate from his friends, and I've never been to his home … naturally.' She looked away.

'Can you tell me his home address at least? I can

probably find out the rest.'

'That I can help you with. He lives ... *lived* at 36 Victoria Ave, Claremont.'

I took out my phone and keyed the address into my memos. 'Wife's name?'

'Stacey Jane,' she said quietly. 'They have two children, Maria and Armanno. Only Maria lives at home.'

'How old is Maria?'

'Sixteen.'

That was enough to get me started. I patted her awkwardly on her shoulder. 'Now what's your address.'

She gave it to me, and as I typed it in I said, 'Wal will be with you first thing in the morning. Now go home and get some rest, Phoebe. Try not to worry.'

She straightened, stood up and gave me a watery smile. 'I'm grateful I ran into you yesterday, Tara. I badly needed a friend and the universe sent me one.'

My heart expanded a little, and I shut the guilt out. 'I'll do what I can.'

I showed her to the door and locked up after she drove away. As I made my way up to bed, I realised that the ant bites had almost stopped hurting.

A quick glance into Cass's room told me she'd beaten me to light out. I lay down on my bed amid the sea of unpacked clothes and strewn shoes. Sleep couldn't come quickly enough.

Chapter 18

I woke to daylight and the delicious smell of bacon wafting up from the kitchen.

'Cass?' I yelled out.

When she didn't reply, I pulled my jeans on under my nightie and wandered downstairs to see what was cooking.

Cass was busy scrambling eggs over one of the two large stoves and Wal was sitting up on one of the three kitchen benches that lined the walls, drumming his booted heels on the cupboards.

In the middle was a fourth large, square bench that served as a kitchen table or a giant chopping block. We had no stools.

'Smells good,' I said, eyeing the dried herbs she was sprinkling into the eggs. 'Where'd you learn to do that?'

'Everyone can fry bacon and scramble eggs,' said Cass over her shoulder. Her hair was scraped back into a pony tail and she wore shorts and a crumpled Megadeth t-shirt.

Everyone except me.

'Wal,' I said, ignoring her bait. 'We've got a job. I need you to watch Phoebe Kenilworth until I can find out who's harassing her and why.'

'The Premier's daughter?'

'Yep.'

'Won't she have ... like cops around her?'

'She doesn't live at home, and this is something she wants to keep quiet,' I said checking my phone. I forwarded her address to Wal's number. 'Can you go now?'

He glanced mournfully across at the eggs. 'After breakfast?'

My stomach rumbled in agreement. 'After breakfast.'

The three of us stood around the centre bench, forking our eggs onto some crusty fresh bread, and crunching the bacon.

'You've shopped,' I said.

'It's our first day in our new house. Wanted us to start it properly.'

'How'd you pay?' I asked.

'You left your purse downstairs. Change is on the counter.'

I sighed and raised my eyebrows to Wal, but he just grinned and went to rinse his plate.

When he'd gone, Cass and I cleaned up and went over our schedule. She was going to work and then class. I was going to visit the Romeos, have lunch with Ed to explain why I was at the parade with someone else, and then check in on Garth. So far nothing in my day held any appeal.

I dropped Cass at work about a half hour later and did a drive by the Romeos' house. It turned out they lived almost dead opposite Aunt Liv's apartment block but on the river side.

I couldn't see any cops or paparazzi, so I parked and walked up to the security gate and buzzed. While I was still working up a story in my head, Maria Romeo's face appeared on the screen. I knew it had to be her from the familiar teenage scowl.

'Your mum home?' I asked.

'Who are you?' Her voice sounded thin through the intercom.

'I'm a private investigator,' I said, deciding to go with only a slight stretch of the truth. 'I'm very sorry for your loss. Would I be able to speak with her?'

'Mum doesn't want to talk to anyone like you. And you'd best leave before my brother hears you. He'll likely knock you sideways.'

'This could be important. About your father,' I said.

She killed the video feed anyway.

Right. Not the way I'd imagined it going.

I went back to Mona and sat staring at the picture of Phoebe and her stalker on my phone. Recognition lingered frustratingly just outside my grasp, so I texted the image to both my cousin Crack and Lloyd Honey. Lloyd was an ex-client of mine who had access to lots of personal information about people. I didn't ask how and he did me the odd favour on account of the service I'd once done him. One day that payback would probably run out, but for the moment, Lloyd seemed happy enough to help when he could.

Crack answered almost immediately with a negative. While I waited for Lloyd to answer, I grabbed my binoculars out of the glove box and walked across the road to Liv's. I was betting her apartment had a fantastic view into the Romeos' back yard.

I'd had keys to Liv's apartment for years and I let myself in quietly. The place smelled of her Lanvin eau de parfum and I stood for a moment, inhaling her scent, think of the woman who'd been so kind and accepting of me over the years. Without Liv ...

My eyes moistened and I thought of Cass. She needed me the way I'd needed Liv. I mustn't let her down no matter how annoying her teenage self could be.

I went to the window and braced the binoculars against the frame. There was nothing happening in the Romeos' front yard, but at the back there were people by the pool. One appeared to be sullen Maria, who was now sprawled on lounge chair; the others—a thickset dark-haired woman and dark-haired young man—were engaged in an energetic conversation. At this distance and magnification, their auras were impossible to read, but it was easy enough to see that they were disagreeing about something.

After a few moments, the young man went back inside. I watched for a bit longer, but the binoculars began to get heavy.

Just as I was about to pack them away, the automatic garage door lifted, and he—Armanno, I was guessing—got into a blue BMW.

I shoved the binoculars into their case and ran for the door. Following him seemed the next best option I had.

By the time I pulled Mona out onto Victoria Ave, Armanno was rounding the corner towards Queenslea. I sped up and caught him at the highway lights. From there, it was a difficult shadow along the highway and up Thomas St to Leederville. Armanno was one of those drivers who accelerated in spurts, making following him tricky. I hadn't done a lot of car surveillance before, but I did my best to stay a few cars back out of his direct rear view.

Finally, he turned left into Newcastle Street and pulled up just short of the Leederville Hotel. I watched him disappear into the opening between the hotel and its adjacent garden restaurant. Though the gate was open, the hotel wasn't which meant I'd be conspicuous if I wandered in after him.

I sat for a moment, trying to think of a way in when a truck pulled up and began unloading crates of boutique beer to take inside.

I jumped out of Mona and ran across the street to the driver.

'Twenty bucks to help you carry the crates in,' I said to him.

He stared at me for a moment, confused. Then he shook his head. 'Health and Safety says you don't. You're not insured.'

'I also don't work for you if it's cash. Forty bucks. Just one crate.'

I could see him wavering.

'Fifty,' I said. 'Just tell me where to take it.'

He held out his hand. 'Up front.'

I took the note out of my pocket and slapped it in his palm. He tucked it on his hip pocket and slid a crate out for me. 'In there you'll see a cool room right in front of you. Our beer is on the left. Just stack it on top.'

'Cheers.'

I accepted the crate, which was heavier than I expected and headed into the space between premises. It was connected by a pergola and a corrugated plastic roof. Not exactly tasteful but effective.

To the left I saw the cool room, to the right were the restrooms, and in the middle, white tables and chairs, potted palms, and a small bar.

The dark-haired young man leaning on the bar looked about the right size and shape for Armanno. He was leaning into the ear of another man that I recognised as

Phoebe's guy, Mr Short Round. Now I was closer, I could see the latter had thick shoulders and a large gut. His face was also heavily fleshed, like his cheeks might burst if someone squeezed it. Neither of them took any notice of me as I entered the cool room with the beer.

I paused inside the door and listened, but heard nothing. I had to get closer. After shelving the crate, I walked out confidently and straight up to them. 'You think I could get a glass of water?'

Both of them scowled at me but only Phoebe's guy replied. 'Bar's closed.'

I frowned back at them, letting them know their inhospitable manner annoyed me. It also gave me time to take in their auras. Armanno's was a racy blue, tinctured with puddles of black, not uncommon for someone who was grieving. Phoebe's guy was blood red and spotted white, suggesting health issues and dark appetites. It wasn't as pustulant as Johnny Viaspa's aura, but it had a familiar reek.

'Right,' I said. 'I'll go and use the tap in the Ladies then.'

Both of them turned away from me as I walked the couple of steps to the restroom. It was much closer to the bar than the cool room, and by leaving the door a little ajar I could hear some of their conversation.

'… Kenilworth … bitch …'

'… today at …'

'… pay in product …'

The exchange finished there and footsteps told me that Armanno had left.

I flushed one of the toilets, rinsed my hands and headed out. Phoebe's guy didn't look up from the till, and I left as quickly as I could, passing the truck driver on his way in with a load.

'Thanks,' I said softly to him.

He paused for a moment, causing me to stop too. 'Don't know what you're up to love, but you're playing with the wrong people.' He nodded at Phoebe's guy.

'You know his name?' I asked.

He shrugged. 'Everyone calls him Freddie the Frog.'

I smiled, wondering if he was joking.

But he shook his head. 'Believe me, he ain't funny.'

I nodded. 'Thanks. See you.'

Soon as I was back in Mona, I texted the nickname to Lloyd Honey. Maybe it would help.

What did they mean about 'tonight' and 'pay in product'?

I rang Wal. 'Has Phoebe got anything on today or tonight?'

'Apparently, yeah. She's opening some health club in South Freo around lunchtime.'

'Let me know the address. And stick close to her, Wal.

I think something might be going to happen.'

'You find out anything?'

'Maybe … soon,' I said, sending out a prayer to Lloyd Honey.

I hung up and thought about my next immediate problem, which was Ed. I hadn't come up with an explanation that wouldn't be a lie, and I wasn't ready to tell him about Tozzi. I mean, they'd met a few times, but that was all.

Then a brainwave hit me.

I limbered up my thumbs and sent Ed a fresh message.

Ed, I have to go to the opening of a new gym? Can you please come with, and we can talk/eat afterwards. I'll pick u up at 12pm. T x

His reply was almost immediate, as if he'd been waiting for me.

Pick me up from my place.

I started the engine, but Cass called me before I could pull out onto the road.

'Pete's been in here and left you a burner,' she said.

'How does he know where you work?'

She hesitated then managed to spit out the truth. 'I told him.'

'Cass!'

'It's OK, Tara. He's OK. Do you want to come and get it? I have to go. I'm on my break.'

I sighed. 'No. Yes. I'll be there in ten.'

Who'd have thought parenting would be so tough!

Nine minutes later I was outside the deli, watching Cass through the window. She was serving a lady I recognised from Joanna's book club. I waited until the transaction was complete and the lady had left before I went inside.

Cass spotted me immediately and with a sly wink slid the phone across the counter. I took it without a word and sought refuge in Mona.

The phone rang twice before it was answered.

'Bon?'

'It's Jake.'

'J-Jake S-Stranger?'

'What have you found out?' he asked.

'Bon said I have until tomorrow.'

'Sooner is better. I saw you talking to her last night.'

'Tomorrow,' I said firmly. 'I'm still working on it.' Today was a day of buying time.

He paused for a second then said, 'Tomorrow then. There is a number programmed into this phone. Use it to call once. Then chuck it. By the way, nice dress. When we go out on a date, I want you to wear it.'

Did he really just say that? My throat closed over in panic, and I croaked a meaningless noise into the phone.

'Cat got your tongue, Tara?'

I forced a cough and a swallow. 'No,' I managed to say.

'I think the devil has.'

He clicked off with a soft chuckle and left me staring at my phone like it had just poisoned me.

Jeez.

Before I could freak out too much more, Garth rang.

'Can you come to the boutique's warehouse? There's a problem.'

'Who's there?' I asked, not wanting to be seen by Johnny Viaspa's sister.

'Just me and Jasmine. Please come quickly.' He sounded scared.

'Sure. Soon. Hang tight. Where is it?'

'601 Stubbs Terrace, Shenton Park. Come around the back to the loading bay.'

'Be there soon,' I said.

I shot Wal a text telling him what I was doing.

He replied right away with instructions of how to get into the 'bag' he kept locked in his cupboard.

That was Wal-code for his weapons stash.

Australia wasn't a gun society in the way of some other countries. Sure, you could buy them with the right permits, but there were checks and balances in place. And like any modern society there were plenty of illegal ones around. I didn't own, or wish to own a pistol, but I understood the message that Wal was sending me.

Once I stepped into the light and Johnny Viaspa made a connection with me investigating his sister's business, the recent enforced truce I'd been experiencing would likely dissolve. He'd tried to have me killed once. He would try again if I started getting in his way.

Seeing him last night at the parade, was already too much of a red flag.

I didn't feel good going to a warehouse owned by the Viaspa's without some way of defending myself, but going to Wal's first would take time and Garth sounded freaked.

I remembered the tyre iron in the boot and decided that would have to do.

Fifteen minutes later, after two drive-bys to make sure there was no sign of Viaspa, I parked the car a street away and walked down the driveway to the loading dock. The large sliding doors were locked, but Garth was standing in the doorway looking out for me.

I jumped up onto the ramp, clutching my tyre iron, and followed him into the dark space that my eyes registered as being packed with shadowy shapes.

'No lights?' I said quietly.

He took my arm to urge me along, but I resisted until he answered. The hairs on my body were snapped to attention.

'We don't want anyone to know we're here,' he said.

'Then, why are you?'

He tugged insistently. 'Come and see.'

I shook him off, but followed him between towering stacks of boxes that came into sharper focus as my eyes adjusted to the gloom.

We wove our way to somewhere near the centre of the building where Jasmine was standing staring into a large open crate. It was full of mannequins bent at odd angles to fit the confines of the box.

'So?' I said, wanting only to get the hell out of there. 'What?'

'This is one of the box numbers that isn't on the inventory,' said Garth.

'It took us most of the night to find it, because it was right here in the middle.'

I could hear the fatigue in his voice.

'You've been here all night. It's almost 11AM.'

'After the break in, we both felt we had to know what was going on.'

He leaned forward and lifted the mannequin's torso out, resting it against his own body. With a couple of quick twists, he disengaged the head and reached into the neck cavity.

Even in this half-light I could see the white powder in the plastic bag he'd retrieved. 'Each mannequin is loaded with bags,' he said.

I took the bag and held my phone torch up. 'Coke,' I said unnecessarily. We all knew what it was.

'What do we do, Tara?' Garth's voice trembled, and he reached out to Jasmine, who slipped into his embrace. She looked thin and exhausted, and terrified. 'I told Jasmine we should call you before the police.'

Jeez. 'You did the right thing. Now put it back, go home, and let me think. I'll get back to you soon with a plan.'

'The police are in the plan, aren't they, Tara?' he said.

'They are,' I said. 'For sure. But I just need to make sure you and Jasmine are protected. Let me think over the angles.'

He nodded uncertainly.

'Trust me, Garth. You don't want to be held under suspicion of being involved in drug trafficking. Once the police are involved, they'll take no prisoners. Everyone is a suspect. There might be a way to do this without involving you both.' Or me.

They exchanged glances and he nodded again.

'Now, get the hell out of here. But before you do, where's the office? I want to look through the stock computer.'

'We can help you with that,' said Garth.

'You've been here all night. Go home to bed. Wait for me to call.'

'The office is in the back corner near the forklift,' said Jasmine, speaking in a husky whisper. 'The password is *pradaplease*.'

'Right. Now go!'

I gave them both a gentle shove and waited until I heard the far door clunk shut before I moved. In the still and dark of the large shed, I took some slow, calming breaths. This is not something I'd wanted, but here I was, and I had to deal with it. If Johnny Viaspa had even an inkling that Garth and Jasmine knew about this, they'd be in grave trouble.

I made sure the mannequin crate was sealed again before I threaded my way through the stacks, and past the forklift to the office.

The door was open and the air con rattled and blasted cooler air on my overheated skin. I left the light off, using my torch to negotiate my way around.

While I waited for the computer to boot up, I flashed my torch around. It was a typical warehouse office, faintly dusty with posters blue-tacked to the wall: runway models, hair product headshots, and one of Ed's underwear shots from months ago.

I resisted the urge to rip it down and turned back to the screen. The password worked, and it opened to a screensaver photo of a large family get together at some upscale restaurant: thirty or more people raising their glasses. Johnny Viaspa was front and centre.

I quickly clicked on the file manager. Garth knew far more about invoicing and ordering than I did, so I skipped all the spreadsheets in favour of a quick search through the documents.

The files were mainly letters, with some PDF versions of fashion catalogues saved. After thirty minutes, I gave up. If there was any clue to who they were laundering money through, or who supplied the cocaine, it was well hidden.

I shut the file manager and stared at the screen saver. Time to get out of here before someone came.

I was just about to shut down the computer when my phone buzzed.

'Lloyd?' I whispered.

'Ms Sharp. Have I got you at a bad time?'

'I can't talk all that freely right now, but did you find out who he was?'

'I'm sorry. It's proved more difficult than I expected.'

'Can you explain what that means?'

'My people tell me that the government has put sniffers on our IP address. Our search strings are being monitored as well. I'm afraid I have to be very careful where I look for information.'

'No cracking.'

'No cracking. For the moment. We're working on get arounds.'

'I don't want you in any trouble on my behalf. Forget I even asked.'

'I'm sorry, Ms Sharp.'

'It's Tara, Lloyd. Please don't be. But I have to go. I'll be in touch soon.'

'Take care, Ms Sharp.'

He hung up and left me staring at the screen. *Now*

what? I guess that meant going back to the Leederville Hotel and asking around a bit more.

I leaned forward to click the shutdown command, and my hand froze. In the back row of the photo, between two men with sculpted shoulders and styled hair, was a round face I suddenly recognised.

Freddie the Frog!

I could barely see his face above the person in front of him, but now that I was concentrating on it …

I dived back into the file manager and found the image in the Pictures folder. It was named FAMILY-NEW YEAR-2015.

I quickly closed the computer down, and got the hell out of the building.

On the way back to my car, I called Wal. 'I'm coming to the opening. Just make sure you keep Freddie the Frog away from Phoebe.'

'What did you find out?'

'He's a Viaspa.'

When I hung up from Wal, I was shaking. Freddie was a Viaspa. Freddie was harassing Phoebe. Garth's girlfriend was in business with Viaspa. It felt like their tentacles were everywhere, tightening around me whichever way I turned.

My stomach bubbled hard like a boiling kettle and I thought for a moment I might throw up on my dashboard. Instead, I got the burner phone out of my handbag and called the number on it.

Bon answered this time and I told him what I'd found out and where I was going.

'You did good, Sharp,' he said and hung up.

Chapter 19

I didn't know what that meant, but it gave me some small measure of relief. Enough for me to start the car and drive to Ed's. My heart was still tub-thumping when I knocked on his door.

He opened the door without a smile, looking delectable in dark chinos and a thin black t-shirt made from one of those silky synthetics. His hair was tumble-free today around his shoulders, and an earring glinted in one ear. He looked like a modern day Spanish pirate.

'Hi. Thanks for coming with me to this,' I said.

He nodded and followed me down to the car.

We exchanged pleasantries as we drove to Fremantle, and he asked me about the gym opening.

'It's a work thing,' I said. 'I'm flanking a client who's got some problems that need to be handled discreetly.'

'Don't they all,' he said acerbically.

I took a sideways glance. His expression was still stern.

'Look … about the other night at the parade,' I said,

plunging in. 'It wasn't a date. Nick had tickets, and I had to be there because of this client I'm working for.'

'Where did you get the outfit you were wearing?' he said in a clipped voice.

'What? The fringe thing? Bok sent it over when he heard I was going. He usually helps me out if I have to go to something dressy.'

His shoulders relaxed a little, leaving me confused. What exactly was eating at him?

'I've never seen you dressed like that before.' he said.

'Like what? I wish I'd never worn the damn thing, but *so what if I did*,' I said belligerently.

He blinked, still staring straight ahead.

'For heaven's sake, Ed. What's wrong?'

He turned his head my way. I kept my eyes on the road, but I felt the imaginary heat of his gaze scorching my cheek.

'I don't even know where to start … was it the fact that you didn't call me back, or let me know you were coming to the parade? Or that you were there with someone else, wearing a come-fuck-me dress? Or that you left without saying goodbye? Or that your "not-a-date's" wife caused a scene because *she* clearly thought it was a date. Do you think I'm stupid, Tara?'

I took an even deeper breath, struggling to keep the indignant emotion out of my voice. 'Look Ed, I'm sorry I didn't call you back, but Cass ran away, I moved house, and I had two clients to look after. For the record, I don't think you're stupid. The date with Nick Tozzi was work, and … I can wear *whatever* I damn will like, to *wherever* I damn well like, with *whoever* I damn well like!' I finished with a rush, which left me feeling hot and bothered, and my palms sweaty on the wheel.

Ed went back to staring out of the windscreen and we sat in silence as we headed across the bridge and into Freo.

I wasn't going to apologise any more than I had. His comment about the dress had me too pissed for that.

So the silence persisted until we pulled into the car park of a new building amidst the cute cafés along South Terrace. South Fremantle had a lot going for it these days.

I reefed the keys out of the ignition and grabbed my bag ready to get out when his hand stayed me.

'Tara, I'm sorry. The comment about your dress was out of line. I guess I was … surprised … and well … a bit jealous.' His aura rippled and softened.

My mouth dropped open a little. Until now, I'd never really appreciated how much younger than me Ed was. Guys of his age were able to talk about their feelings. I was used to the Nick Tozzi's of the world, the older generation who would never admit to being jealous.

Ed's honesty disarmed me and my anger cooled. 'Let's talk after this thing is over.'

His hand closed over mine. 'We good, Tara?'

I smiled. 'Sure.' *Were we?*

Inside, the new premises gleamed: a paint-fresh, mirror and chrome-shiny, equipment-heavy workout centre. The beats from the surround speakers were bassy and energetic and the crowd had showed up in bright casual gear. There was a fair bit of young money in this area, and they were dressed to prove it. Waiters flitted about with drinks and sushi bites.

The back half of the main room was raised a foot higher that the front half, and I spied Phoebe in the centre of it standing next to a microphone and podium with a small group of people around her. I couldn't see Wal, but I knew he'd be around somewhere, taking the low-key surveillance approach.

'Let's go closer to the front,' I said to Ed who was helping himself to a beer from a waitperson's tray. He took a sip and fired her a brilliant smile in thanks, which sent her blushing from her neck to nose ring.

I didn't wait for him to answer me, and threaded through the crowd where I found a spot against the wall, almost level with the dais. Now I was closer, I could see that it was Armanno Romeo, his sister, Maria, and a woman who had to be Stacey Jane, their mother, standing with Phoebe.

'You know 'em?' asked a voice next to me.

Wal had sidled up without me noticing.

I turned my mouth to his ear. 'Bernard Romeo's family. Do you think they know Phoebe was his mistress?'

He shrugged. 'This is one of the wife's chain of gyms. Phoebe said she usually opened them because of her ambassador work.'

'Keep an eye out for Freddie.'

'Boss, did you go to my place and check the cupboard?'

'No. I improvised,' I said.

He shook his head in disapproval. 'You gotta start carrying something. Prick has already tried to kill you once.'

'That's why I've got you Wal,' I said lightly.

'It ain't enough,' he said. 'I'm tellin' ya.'

'I can look after myself. You worry about Phoebe.'

He shrugged, slouched off, and a few minutes later Ed replaced him. The lights dimmed and a young, fit looking guy stepped up to the microphone.

'I lost you in the crowd,' Ed whispered.

'You should have asked the waiter with the nose ring. She saw where I went ... wait. Oh no she didn't ... she was too busy looking at you,' I whispered back tartly.

He slipped an arm around me, an anxious look on his face. 'Hey, I thought we were alright. I don't want to—'

I didn't hear the rest because the microphone popped and I suddenly spotted Freddie the Frog in the crowd.

I fumbled for my phone and sent Wal a quick 'heads up' text.

'Have to speak to someone,' I said to Ed. 'Save me a vol au vent.'

While the guy at the microphone went through the

introductions and a sentimental spiel about Bernard Romeo, I threaded through the attentive crowd towards Freddie the Frog. He was wide but short, and I lost sight of him twice when people shifted in front of me.

When I got to the spot where I thought he'd been, he was gone. I looked around and saw Phoebe ready to step up and make her speech.

'As patron of Community Health and the Teen Suicide Lobby, I'd like to thank Mrs Stacey Jane Romeo—'

'Looking for someone?'

I whirled around and found myself face to face with Johnny Viaspa. He wore a tight white t-shirt, jeans and a crocodile smile. The kind crocs have just before they get you in the death roll. His aura pulsed in its usual pussy yellow and drowned me in the smell of vomit.

My throat closed over. This man had tried to have me killed, and I was pretty sure that item was still on his to do list.

He leaned forward and whispered, 'Lost your tongue, bitch?'

Try as I could, I couldn't get a sound out.

'Lemme speak for you then,' he continued. 'Stay away from my sister's business, or you and your accountant fuck will end up ...' he shook his head and wagged his finger in a theatrical gesture.

I felt a rush of pure fury that ripped away my fear and I wound my arm back to punch him as hard as I could.

But before I could unleash, Wal grabbed my fist from behind and held it in his own.

'Fuck off,' he said to Viaspa. 'Or I'll mess you up.'

Viaspa's aura erupted, splashing pus everywhere, and his face whitened. For a moment, I was terrified he might pull a gun. Even here, in the crowd.

But Wal stared him down, cold eyed and steady. His own aura was cobalt and rock hard. Impenetrable.

Mine wasn't faring so well. I could feel swells of heat and cold rolling off me.

'You'll get yours, roadie,' said Viaspa. He turned and strutted away.

The people closest, who saw the interchange, whispered to each other. Aside from that, the crowd remained undisturbed.

Wal took my arm and shepherded me to the very back of the room near the water cooler. The crowd had their backs to us and Johnny Viaspa was nowhere in sight.

'Thanks, Wal,' I said. 'Truly. I would have …'

'He's a bad bit of work,' said Wal calmly. 'You need to carry protection.'

He slipped something cold into my hand.

My fingers close around it. A knife.

'I can't.'

'You will, or I'm going to find you face down in an alley somewhere,' he said bluntly.

'I-I—'

He stared me right in the face. I could smell the Sobranie's on his breath. 'You crossed a line, boss. It's not too late for you to cross back, but you need to move interstate and quit your business. Otherwise ...'

'Face reality. Start carrying protection. Live like someone who's got enemies,' I finished for him.

He nodded. 'Look I've got your back. You're ... well, you're family now. But I'm not going to be with you every minute of every day. And I gotta take care of Liv as well. Your enemies are her enemies.' He ran his fingers through his hair. For the first time ever, I saw the shadow of anxiety creep across his face.

'Well, I promise I'll take precautions. But let's just get through tonight. We have to get Phoebe home safely.'

He nodded. 'Let me get back to her.'

'I'll wait 'til this is over, and follow you home.'

He nodded. 'We'll leave through the back door. I parked close to it. See you in a bit.'

He walked back through the crowd and left me alone.

I sidled over towards the makeshift bar, helped myself to a red wine, and went back to Ed. He was still leaning in the same position that I left him. I settled next to him and tried to listen to the last of the speeches, but the truth was my mind was in nervous overdrive.

Bernard Romeo had been a real estate agent. His wife owned a chain of gyms and he had a mistress who happened to be the Premier's daughter. Freddy the Frog—a

Viaspa—was harassing her to find some list of Bernard's 'clients'. His real estate clients?

Freddy the Frog was also in cahoots with Bernard's son, Armanno. At the same time, Garth had discovered a crate load of synthetic coke over in his girlfriend's clothes warehouse. The same girlfriend who was in business with Johnny Viaspa's sister. The two had to be connected? But how?

Should I call the cops and give them a tip off about the warehouse? Or would Viaspa come after me? He already knew I was helping Garth.

Maybe if I could link him to the drugs, bring him down, then he'd be too busy fending off crown prosecutors with lawyers to worry about who got him busted.

The crowd burst into applause to signal the end of the speeches and the noise level went up. The gym had been officially opened, and some people were already heading for the door.

'You want to go and grab some food in Freo?' said Ed. He slipped his arm around my waist, but I was too tense to relax into it. 'Tara?' he prompted me.

'I told Wal, I'd follow him and our client home. Can we grab a bite after that?'

'Sure. I guess.'

We stood together and talked inconsequential stuff until the last of the guests had left and only the Romeos, the staff, Phoebe, Wal, Ed and I remained.

Ed glanced at the time on the wall clock and then around. 'Can we go? Who's your client?'

Phoebe waved to me right then.

Ed made a strangled noise. 'The Premier's daughter?'

I shrugged. 'We went to school together.'

Phoebe approached looking tired beneath her flawless makeup. Her eyes were a little bloodshot.

'Nice speech,' I said to her. 'This is Eduardo Pote.'

Phoebe extended a hand and her face became more animated.

Ed had that effect on people.

'Lovely to meet you, Eduardo. Tara, I need to get out of here. As you can imagine, it's a little awkward.'

She glanced around as if expecting the Romeos to descend on her.

'Sure. Wal will take you home and Ed and I will follow.'

'This way,' said Wal pointing beyond the dais.

The four of us left the gym through the back door, past a skip bin and some discarded plastic chairs waiting to be tossed out, and walked over to Phoebe's Mercedes Sports. Normally I'd have admired the car, but it was too dark now to see it properly, and I had an anxious feeling in the pit of my stomach that I couldn't explain.

We weren't the only ones using the tradesmen's entrance. The Romeo family appeared behind us in the car park.

Phoebe gave an awkward little farewell wave and beeped her ignition key to unlock the car.

Armanno shouted something in another language and Stacey Jane grabbed his arm. But he flung her off and ran over to the skip bin from which he seized a lump of iron.

'Wal!' I said in warning

As Wal grabbed Phoebe around the waist and swung her off her feet, Armanno charged. At the last moment, Wal stepped lightly sideways and shoved him off balance. I launched forward and knocked Armanno over.

We fell together, me landing heavily on his legs, and he kicked me in the face. He recovered quickly as I recoiled and before Wal could disengage from Phoebe, Armanno was on his feet and smashing the windscreen with the iron bar, screaming, 'bitch-whore!'

'Ed,' I bellowed. 'Stop him!'

Galvanised by my command, Ed grabbed Armanno's arms and wrestled him backwards.

Wal put Phoebe down away from danger and set upon Armanno from the front. First, he prised the iron from his fingers and tossed it away across the car park. Then he wrenched the young man from Ed's grasp and with two fast, efficient punches, one to the groin and one under the jaw, he laid Armanno out on the ground.

The angry young man cried out then rolled over and crawled away towards his mother and sister. The women who were clinging to each other, ran to him.

'Tara, take Phoebe home in your car,' said Wal in a flat voice. 'I'll bring hers once this is sorted.'

'Yes,' I said.

Phoebe hadn't uttered a word through the entire event, and in the dark, I couldn't see her aura. I went over and put my arm around her. She was trembling, and her skin felt hot. Ed joined us and together we steered her to my car.

'Are you alright,' I asked as I sped out of the car park.

'How long have they known?' she answered in a hoarse voice.

'I don't expect that matters right now,' I said. 'What does matter is that the man who's been harassing you is connected with someone dangerous.'

'Dangerous?'

'Let's just say that being the Premier's daughter won't necessarily be enough to protect you.'

She fell silent again for a few moments. The streetlights skidded past and I could see Ed's profile, his chest rising and falling in the flickering of light and shadow. His expression was hard to read.

'There's something I should have told you, Tara,' she said as we turned onto the Freo bridge. 'But I ...' she faded off.

'You can trust Ed,' I said.

'Does he work for you?'

'Yes,' said Ed, before I could answer.

I shot him a sideways look as we pulled up at traffic lights. What?

'I'm bound by her confidentiality agreement,' he added.

It was a whopping lie, but I wasn't about to call him on it right now.

'What is it, Phoebe?'

'I know what the man wants from me. It's a list. Perhaps you can negotiate an exchange? If they leave me alone, you can give it to them.'

I thought about it for a moment. 'His nickname is Freddy the Frog. What's on the list? And where is it?'

'Names. They didn't mean anything to me. It's in my beach apartment in Swanbourne.'

I wanted to say *you have a beach apartment*, but settled for, 'Why the change of heart? I thought you hired me to avoid having to deal with him?'

A motorbike changed lanes right in front of me and I hit the brakes hard to avoid a collision. To my annoyance, it then accelerated away leaving us behind.

'What the fuck …' I muttered under my breath.

'I don't like being intimidated,' Phoebe said. 'I thought maybe you could find out something about them that could make it all go away. But whatever Bernie gave me, he's gone, and it's not worth risking my life over.'

'That's smart. I'm just going to drop Ed home then we might take a look at the list.'

'Yes,' said Phoebe.

'I'll come too,' said Ed.

'No. It's fine. You have to work early. I'll call you

tomorrow so we can talk.'

'Promise,' he said quietly.

I nodded.

None of us spoke again until I pulled to the kerb outside Ed's apartment. He and I got out of the car to speak.

'You want to come back after you've dropped her home?' he asked softly.

I shook my head. 'Tonight's been a bit rough,' I said. 'Let's do something soon though.'

'I meant what I said about working for you,' he said. 'I meet a lot of people. I could be kind of ... you know ... undercover or something. A source.'

'You're serious?' I asked, surprised.

'As a church in Lent.'

'Well that's a conversation for another day.' I leaned forward and kissed him. 'Call me when you're free.'

He pulled me closer and hugged me tight. 'Please be careful.'

'Always,' I said.

Chapter 20

Phoebe's 'beach apartment' turned out to be down the south end of Cottesloe. As we drove up the steep street from the sea, I recognised the huge old vacant house in front of her block. My grandmother had lived for a while in a flat on the next cross street, and as a kid I'd always wanted to play in the empty yard.

Granna had insisted the building was dangerous and that the property was private. Even so, I'd snuck in there once or twice and peeked in the windows. If I'd believed in ghosts, I would have been sold on them living in the 'big' house; as it was, it always gave me a prickling sensation all over skin. Even now ...

'There,' said Phoebe.

She pointed to a gate securing the underground car park entrance to her building, and produced a remote from her bag to let us in.

I negotiated the tight space and squeezed Mona in between a Jaguar and a Porsche. We got out and took a ride up three floors in a key-accessed, wood-panelled lift, which opened onto a small foyer with two doors. Phoebe's place—on the right—occupied the entire northern corner of the floor.

Inside, the blinds were open and I could see the outline of the 'big' house in front and the lights of cargo ships out towards Rottnest. From the other window the rest of the suburb blinked comfortingly.

She turned the lights on and I squinted to accommodate the change, taking in a spotless and expensively furnished room. Oversized grey leather armchairs and a black marble bench. The shelves of the well-oiled bookcase sat against one wall, filled with chrome and gilt photo frames of Phoebe on various adventures. There were only a few books. 'You come here much?'

'Weekends. About once a month. Not many people know about it.' She walked over to the bench and ran her fingers along it. 'Bernie used to come here sometimes. The car park and lift made it easy to be discrete. You want a drink?'

'Sure,' I said. 'What have you got?'

She opened the fridge and retrieved a bottle of champagne. 'I'd been saving it, but you know … there's no point now …'

I waited while she popped the cork, found some glasses and settled into one of the armchairs. She drank quickly and I was patient enough to take a couple of sips of the slightly bitter fizz before I said, 'So this list of names …?'

'Oh yes,' she said as if she'd forgotten. She put down her glass and went over to a light fitting on the wall. The watermarked white shade was shaped like a half moon and with a gap at the top to insert the bulb.

Phoebe fished around inside it and produced a memory stick. 'Here.'

'Can we have a look?'

I could see now that the champagne had already unwound her a bit and she seemed exhausted. She dragged herself to the desk bureau set in front of the north window and plugged the stick into a thin, lightweight hybrid tablet.

'All yours,' she said when the document opened. She returned to the chair and poured herself another glass.

I was only halfway through mine but I could feel it loosening the tightness in my muscles as well.

My phone rang and I answered it as I perused the list.

'Where are you?' said Wal in a terse voice.

'Jeez, sorry. In Phoebe's beach apartment in South Cott. I have the—'

'Sit tight.' He cut me off deliberately.

I paused. 'Wal?'

'Don't leave. Got it? Make sure everything's locked. I'm on my way, but I have to make a detour.'

'Wal? Should I be—?'

But he'd hung up.

I glanced over at Phoebe. She had her head resting on

the arm of the chair, eyes closed.

I took the wine glass out of her hand and put it on the table. Then I went and checked the doors and windows, and drew the blinds. Once my eyes accustomed to the near-dark, I went back and peeped out. There was nothing to see other than the outline of the 'big' house in front.

Closing my eyes, I drew a mind picture of the contours of the garden: how it was terraced at the back, and how the weeds and grass had overtaken everything making it hard to see one step from another. I remembered the old water tank, rusted through in places and a gardening shed that was still standing, but barely. I'd hidden in that shed once, away from a boy who'd followed me back from the beach. An INXS song had been blaring on the radio on the building site of what was now Phoebe's apartment block. Every time I heard that song afterwards, I still remembered the faint scent of dry potting mix, and the mixture of fear and excitement in my stomach as the boy passed by without a clue that I was hiding there.

I went back to reading the screen. Only one, on the list of nine names, seemed familiar. Jeff Tyler. If it was the same guy I knew, I'd dated his older brother Craig for a month when I was seventeen. Jeff had been a scrawny, annoying, smart-mouthed younger sibling, who'd perved on us in the back seat of their parents' car.

I opened the browser and googled his name. It gave me thousands of hits. I added Perth into the search string and went to Google Images, which gave me a better result.

He popped up in a few places. I fancied I could see the same sulky mouth and sly eyes in the muscled and tanned photos of a Jeff Tyler at the state body building championships.

Who'd have thought it?

I got up and paced a little. Phoebe was breathing lightly, her mouth open and one arm flung over her head. She looked more sixteen than twenty-six.

I wandered over to the bookcase and ran my fingers along the tops of the photo frames. Phoebe was a beautiful woman, especially when she laughed. I liked one in particular, taken on a beach. She was toasting the camera with a glass of champagne, dressed in a flowing see-through shirt over bikinis. The sun was low in the sky and she looked so carefree. She'd stuck a little caption in the corner of the photo with the date. New Year's Eve last. Was Bernard the one taking the picture? Had he made her that happy?

I sighed. Where *was* Wal? He should be here by now.

I sent Cass a text; telling her not to wait up because I might be home late; to make sure all the perishable food she'd bought got unpacked into the fridge; and to lock the doors. Then I sent one to Garth, checking in and saying I'd call him in the morning and he wasn't to worry.

Somehow the texts settled me a bit. Structure. Panning. Normality. My thoughts turned to the puzzle in front of me. Both Johnny Viaspa and the Western Cheaters wanted this list of names. Why? Who were these people?

I went back into the kitchen, picked up my bag and pulled out the knife Wal had given me. How badly did they want it?

My phone buzzed. 'Garth?'

'Tara, I know you said we'd sort it out tomorrow, but that ... thing we saw earlier ... I think there might some movement.'

'What do you mean?'

'Tonight. We can see lights inside and a four-wheel drive parked near the back door. We think it's being moved.'

'You mean you're outside?'

'We were worried. We thought we should—'

'I told you to go home. Don't go near it. Alright?'

'But ...'

'I've never been more serious about anything, Garth,' I said. 'I'll deal with it.'

I hung up. If they were shifting the coke tonight, now, I had to call the cops. Which meant that I needed a burner phone.

There was an all-night deli on the next block. They would have one.

I called Wal, to ask him to stop and pick one up, but he didn't answer. How long would he be? It wouldn't take them long to move the coke, depending on whether they were dividing it there, or taking it somewhere else. I had to act now.

A quick check on Phoebe told me she'd moved into a more comfortable position, her face pressing into the back of the chair. Her slumber seemed deeper, more restful.

I grabbed my handbag and her remote, and the door key she'd dropped in a bowl by the door. I went to let myself out, then turned back and grabbed the memory stick. Once I'd tucked it in my jeans pocket, I headed to the lift.

Outside was quiet. Only a few cars parked on the street; most people hunkered down in front of their screens for the night. I jogged down a block to the deli and bought the last burner phone he had in stock.

He slid it across the counter and I tore the packing open then and there.

'Everything alright, Miss,' he asked politely.

'Fine,' I said. 'Dropped my phone in the bath. Need to cancel a dinner date.'

'Aaaah,' he smiled. 'Another broken heart.'

'Something like that,' I said forcing a grin.

A customer came in looking for cigarettes and I took the opportunity to step out.

I stopped at the nearest stormwater grate I could find and rang the cops while I knelt down and cleared debris from the grill.

'There something strange going on in a warehouse

halfway down Stubbs Terrace, Shenton Park. I think it might be a something to do with drugs. But it's happening right now. You should send someone right away,' I said in a fake voice.

I hung up before they could ask me any questions, ripped the sim card out, and dropped it in the drain. Then I wiped the phone with my shirt sleeve and went in search of a rubbish bin to toss it into.

I spotted a solo bin on the verge of the house about halfway back to Phoebe's, but across the road. If I remembered correctly from when Granna was here, rubbish would be collected tomorrow, and the phone would be buried in refuse at the tip.

I crossed the street towards it, wondering about some of the decisions I'd made lately. As I did, a car pulled away from the kerb without its lights on and drove straight at me.

I barely had time to pitch myself sideways, and it caught me on the hip, sending me sprawling onto the bitumen. While I rolled in agony, the car pulled into a driveway and reversed out. I grabbed my handbag, and rolled towards the kerb.

The whole thing had occurred almost silently. Maybe I'd shouted in pain. I didn't know. No one came out to see what had happened.

And now the driver was coming back for a second pass. I scrambled to my feet. My hip hurt so badly I felt faint, but forced myself to stay conscious and keep moving, hustling along the sidewalk.

But the car wasn't giving up so easily and it mounted.

I saw it coming and jumped over a low brick fence into someone's yard where one leg folded beneath me. The car braked short of the obstacle and waited there to see my next move.

'Can you walk?' said a voice in my ear.

My racing heart almost exploded and I instinctively lashed out. But a hand caught mine, and held it fast in a way that was familiar.

'Wal?' I breathed.

'It's me.'

'You could have led with that,' I said. 'Yes, I can walk, but not sure how far.'

'Run?'

'A little. Maybe. Depends. Who's in the car?'

'Viaspa, or one of his,' said Wal.

'Can't we just go and knock on someone's door for help.'

'Not unless you want them shot.'

'That's ridiculous. They're not going to shoot a member of the public.'

'Take a look at the roof of the car.'

I peered at the dark outline of the car and saw nothing. 'Where?'

'Look at the bonnet.'

I squinted more and saw a figure hunched forward over the hood. 'What's he doing?'

'Move!' said Wal and rolled me right into a garden bed of weeds just as I heard a short, sharp whoosh.

'What was that? I whispered.

'Silencer.'

'*He just shot at me?*'

'Come on!'

Wal was crawling backward alongside the porch, heading for the side of the house. I followed him as quickly as my hip would allow and encountered a narrow side corridor of the garden filled with pot plants and bordered by a tall colorbond fence.

When we were out of sight of the car, he gestured upward. 'Get over the fence and back to Phoebe.'

'What are you going to do?'

'Call the cops and try and keep the shooter away.'

'What do you mean?'

'Trust me, it's about to get a lot worse.'

'Wal?'

'Whatever they want, it's important. The Cheaters have been trailing you. They're here as well.'

'The Cheaters will protect us.'

'In theory, maybe,' he said. 'But it's dark, and shit happens.'

My adrenalin levels spiked again. 'Shit,' I said. 'I have what they want. It's a list of names.'

'What names?'

'I only recognised one of them, Jeff Tyler.'

'Tylenol?'

'You know him too.'

'He's a dealer. Steroids. Where's this list?'

'In my back pocket.'

'Give it to me. Quick.'

'I don't know that's such a good—'

'They catch you with it, they'll cut out your tongue for it. If you're lucky.'

I fished it out of my pocket and handed it over. Wal lifted the base of the heavy pot we were squatting next to.

'You'll crush it.'

'Hopefully,' he said. 'Now go.'

He interlaced his fingers as a sling, and I put my foot in them. But his boost got me up top of the fence just as the front porch light came on, silhouetting me against the night.

I immediately dived down the other side, hearing the same soft thunk, whizzing past me. Levering onto my knees, I realised that I'd fallen onto a grassy easement between neighbour's fences. Then the car engine started up and headlights blinded me.

'Wait!' I said holding up my hands. 'I've got what you want.'

Nothing happened, but I was still alive, so I began to walk towards the car.

'Everything alright out there?' called a querulous older woman's voice from the porch.

I didn't dare answer in case he pulled the trigger on me.

'Fine. Just a lover's quarrel,' said the voice from behind the car's headlights.

'Can you please turn those lamps off, young man? You're waking the street.'

I stepped closer, still unable to see my pursuer.

'Sure thing, ma'am,' said the guy.

The porch light dimmed and I took another step. I was almost at the bonnet of the car, when a bunch of things happened: Wal appeared from the side and tackled the shooter who was focussed on me; two motorbikes turned the corner near the deli and accelerated towards us; and another car roared down the street from the north.

'Run!' bellowed Wal. He had the shooter guy on his back, hands around his neck. I stood, indecisive for a moment, then common sense kicked in. Wal could take care of himself, but not if he had me to worry about as well.

My hip throbbed with pain as I hurtled towards Phoebe's. But I saw another car in her driveway, lights on, idling, so I veered off at the last second down towards the 'big' house.

Once through the gap in the fence, I crashed through the undergrowth trying to get my bearings.

Car doors slammed shut close by.

Loud gunshots rang out.

I navigated the pitch-black yard towards the water tank on memory, feeling thankful I knew about it. When my fingers touched its cool iron, I followed its contour until they caught the jagged edge of a rusted-out hole. I pulled hard, and broke a large section of the corrugation away. It left enough of a hole for me and I climbed in, praying that I didn't disturb a nest of brown snakes.

The tank was deep with wet leaves, and I squatted in them catching my breath.

Then I called Phoebe.

She answered after two rings.

'It's Tara,' I whispered. 'Don't answer the door to anyone, and don't come outside.'

'What's happening? Where are you? I heard shots.'

'I'm OK. Wal's called the police. Sit tight.'

'Tara—'

As I hung up, the leg holding up my sore hip cramped and gave way beneath me again. Only the sound of more gunshots stopped me from crying out.

Was it the Cheaters shooting? Or Viaspa? Or Wal? Or were they shooting at each other? What the hell was going on? This was the suburbs. They couldn't just have a gunfight.

They couldn't ju—

'Saw you come in here, bitch. Hand over the list.' Viaspa's distinctive voice came from somewhere in the yard. He must have been in the second car.

I held my breath. Maybe hiding in the tank wasn't such a good idea. If he looked in here … it'd be like shooting fish in a barrel.

Then I remembered Wal's knife and felt for it in my bag.

Could I really stab someone?

Another deep breath. If it was Viaspa, yes. I could.

I pressed against the tank wall and edged a bit closer to the opening.

The light from his mobile phone bounced around as he searched for me.

'I'm close, Tara,' he carolled.

Where were the police? Wal? Sweat ran in rivulets down the back of my legs. If it was true that you could smell fear then I knew I was stinking up the place.

Then light found the tank and Viaspa knocked on the outside of it right where I was crouched. 'You in the tank, *Sharp?*'

I gripped the knife tighter truly in danger of fainting now. Maybe if I burrowed down he wouldn't see me. But being this close, he'd hear, I argued with myself.

He knocked on the tank every few seconds, as if he was testing for holes. A few more steps and he'd find the one that I'd widened. A few more seconds and I'd have to plunge this knife into his flesh.

I raised it ready to strike, two shaking hands holding the hilt.

Fuck. Fuck. Fuuck.

'Boss,' another voice called. 'The cops have turned onto Eric Street. Let's go.'

'She's here. I know she is.'

'Boss! We've got word. We need to go now.'

Viaspa swore. Then the torch light changed direction.

A few seconds later, car doors slammed shut, and they drove off.

I collapsed back into the leaves and lay there trembling. When I recovered enough to feel my feet and hands again, I tried texting Wal. But he didn't reply.

I couldn't deal with what that might mean so I stayed where I was, not daring to risk going back to Phoebe's while the police cordoned off the street and knocked on doors.

I sent her a text instead.

I'm OK. Stay inside. Keep everything locked. Will call you tomorrow.

Around daybreak, everything had gone quiet except for the sound of the council rubbish truck working its way up and down the streets. I emerged from the tank, plastered in leaves, and hobbled up the hill. Bright yellow police tapes were up in the easement near where I'd crouched and there were chalk marks on the bitumen.

No one was around, so I hobbled slowly down Phoebe's

driveway. I was just about to use the remote to open the screen when a figure detached itself from behind the brick letterbox on the verge.

'Tara?' said Detective Fiona Bligh.

She startled me so badly that I stumbled and fell backwards. Next thing I knew, she was leaning over me, lightly slapping my cheek.

'What on earth's wrong with you, Sharp?'

I sat up and burst into tears.

Bligh was in jeans and a t-shirt. She produced a Kleenex from her pocket.

'What are y-you still doing h-here?' I gulped into the tissue.

'I'm the one asking the questions. There's been a shootout overnight in South Cottesloe. Why am I not surprised to see you? And why do you look like you've done ten rounds with a whipper snipper?'

I gulped a few more times until the storm of emotion began to settle. The rubbish truck roared up from the beach side and then braked to collect the bins that had been left out. I watched it thoughtfully.

'Is there somewhere we can talk?' I asked.

'Step into my office.' She offered me a hand and pulled me up. Then with an altogether way too firm grip on my arm, she shepherded me behind the rubbish truck and over to an unassuming sedan in one of the cross streets.

'Shake off some of those leaves,' she said and stood

watching me do it.

I dusted myself off as well as I could and then she popped the locks. It took a moment to manoeuvre myself into the passenger seat. My hip was now stiff as well as painful. She got into the driver's seat and twisted sideways to look me over.

'So, you're a detective now? Or just off duty?' I asked.

'Both. I attended the trouble last night and offered to stick around until the day shift came on.'

'Why'd you do that?'

She arched her eyebrows. 'I looked through the list of tenants in the street. Phoebe Kenilworth lives in one of those apartments.'

'So?' I said.

'She's connected with the floater you're acquainted with. But you already know that, don't you?'

'Can you read minds?' I asked faintly.

She smiled—just a little bit. Her aura was normally streaked with grey, but this morning the streaks looked more like puffs of grey clouds. Like me, she was tired. 'To a degree. And now you're going to tell me what I *don't* know.'

I'd been dreading this situation since the moment Garth rang me. A face to face with the police. Yet if it had to be anyone, I'm glad it was Bligh. And I intended to keep it that way.

'I'm only talking to you,' I said. 'No negotiation.'

She nodded. 'I'm touched.' A hint of sarcasm too. 'Now tell me.'

'Phoebe Kenilworth hired me to investigate some guy who was harassing her. He seemed to think she had something of Bernard Romeo's that was valuable.'

'What thing?'

'Information on a USB drive.'

'What kind of information?'

'I don't know.'

'So this … dust-up last night … the parties involved were hoping to secure this USB?'

'I imagine so.'

'We spoke to Phoebe Kenilworth. She didn't mention any of this. No one had been near her door. No one attempted to break in. How did you come to be out on her street?'

'I dropped her home from an opening. She let me park underneath. Then I went out to the deli on the corner to buy a cheap phone because I needed to make a call and my phone had gone dead.'

'Why didn't you use Phoebe's?'

'I don't make a habit of using my client's phones. It's unprofessional.'

'Where's the phone now?'

I watched the rubbish truck turn the corner and disappear from view.

'Same place as the thumb drive I guess.'

'Meaning?'

'I had the thumb drive on me when I went to the shop. Safe keeping. Phoebe wouldn't have mentioned it because she didn't want her association with Romeo to be public knowledge. Everyone knows that the police can't keep a secret.'

'I'll ignore that. Why were you driving Phoebe anywhere?'

'Her car met with an accident.'

Bligh's eyebrows lifted, and a gleam of comprehension lit her eyes.

'Armanno Romeo attacked it?'

'How do you know that?'

'The caretaker for the offices next door saw it all. He called it in. We ran the plates on the cars involved.'

'Jeez.'

'Back to this information, Sharp. Where is it?'

'I don't know. I had it in my pocket with my disposable phone. They must have fallen out when I hid in the rainwater tank. Can't find it now.'

'You lost the disposable phone and the thumb drive, but managed to somehow keep hold of your own phone? How fortunate.'

'I was in a bit of a state, you know.'

'Sharp?' she said fixing me with a quizzical stare. 'Is that the truth?'

'I've spent all night in a tank filled with muck and

leaves after being shot at by persons unknown. Of course, it is.' I sold the lie with a slightly frustrated shake of my head.

'So, we should be thanking you for keeping the Premier's daughter safe?'

I shrugged. 'I don't need thanking. I need a shower.'

'And you have no idea what was on the thumb drive?'

'No.'

'Phoebe hadn't looked at it?'

'Not as far as I know.' I figured that would stack up if they questioned Phoebe further. She'd been asleep when I'd scanned the list. She couldn't rightfully say I'd seen it. And I don't think she had.

'Yet another convenience' she said.

'I'm itchy. Can I go home please?'

'I'll need a statement first.'

I sighed. Didn't she always?

Chapter 21

Wal was waiting for me in the kitchen at home when I got back from the cop shop around 7AM. His grey aura was fuzzy with fatigue. Cass, thankfully, was still asleep upstairs.

I wasn't sure who was more relieved to see the other. We huddled in the kitchen over the kettle and watched it boil while I told him my version first.

'Way to handle it, boss,' he said when I was done. 'Enough of the truth but not too much.'

'But now I have to go back and get the thumb drive before the police start searching for it.

He pulled his cigarette packet out of his pocket, turned it on its side and gave it a tap. A black USB slid out.

I stared, open mouthed. Then I gave him a relieved smile. 'Now tell me what happened to you.'

'I went at it with the shooter for a bit, 'til I knew you'd gone and the Cheaters turned up. Figured it was time to keep a low profile then. Hid in an empty dog kennel until about 4AM. Got the USB back and climbed through back yards and over fences all the way back to the beach. Walked up to Swanbourne end then home.'

'That must've taken hours.'

'A while,' he allowed.

I took two cups out of the drainer and plonked teabags in them. Cass had not only arranged the crockery and cutlery, but we miraculously now seemed to own a tea and a sugar caddy, pearly white and striped blue. 'But the place was crawling with cops all night.'

'Only seen one left there when shift changed. She was camped near the letterbox out front of the client's block.'

'That was Fiona Bligh.' I picked my bag up off the counter and retrieved Wal's knife. 'Thought I was going to have to use it.'

'Viaspa?'

'He was so close to me, Wal.' I shuddered. 'I swear he knew I was there. If the cops hadn't arrived when they did.'

'You keep that,' he said.

I gave a reluctant nod and put it back in my bag. 'I don't want to ever use it. But it might give me a fighting chance if I had to.'

We sipped our tea in silence for a bit.

'What do you think the list is for?' I asked.

Wal glanced over at the door as if making sure no one had snuck in to the room unannounced. 'Dealers network would be my guess. That Romeo bloke must have been shifting some kind of product. The list'll be his people.'

I had a flash of intuition. 'Of course. He's been selling through his wife's gyms.'

Wal squinted and started filling the electric kettle. 'Makes sense. Maybe the Cheaters and Viaspa *both* want it. The territories for selling are pretty organised. Viaspa deals coke. The Cheaters sell pot and amphetamines. Maybe one of them is making a move on the other.'

'Or they're looking to take on a different product entirely,' I said.

Wal switched on the kettle and then suddenly thumped the counter. ''Roids and EPO.'

'Performance enhancers?'

'Maybe Romeo's had the monopoly for selling that kind of juice in the state. Now he's dead, the others want to take over his patch.'

I nodded with sudden energy. 'That's it Wal! It would also explain Armanno Romeo's connection with Freddie the Frog. He was hoping to take over from his dad. Maybe he was throwing in with Viapsa.' Then I sagged. 'So what do we do with the list? If I don't turn it over to the cops, then the Cheaters and Viaspa will come for us.'

'They'll come for us even if you do turn it over. Unless you fancy a stint in WitPro.'

I shook my head. I did not.

Wal rubbed his cheek, thinking it through. 'But if you

give it the Cheaters, boss, then you'll be done owing them.'

'Or I could just destroy it so no one has the names. Morally, that would be the right thing to do, Wal.' I didn't hold with chemical abuse much outside a few drinks and a Berocca chaser.

Wal shrugged again. 'They'll build it again anyway. The market's too big and lucrative to pass up. But it'll take time. Time is money. They'll kill you for that.'

I shrugged feeling hopeless. 'They're going to kill me anyway. Garth found a stash of synthetic coke at his girlfriend's clothing warehouse.'

'The girlfriend who's in business with Viaspa's sister?'

'Yep. That's her. Garth called me to say they were shifting the gear last night.'

'And?'

'And I made an anonymous call to the cops.'

'Fuck.'

'Yeah.' I nodded miserably.

'Well that makes the choice easy. You have to give the list to the Cheaters in return for protection from Viaspa.'

I shook my head vehemently. 'That's a one-way road to trouble, Wal.'

He came over to me and put his hand on my shoulder. His aura swelled around me like a grey pillow-soft cloud. 'Tara. You're already on that road. Now you have to survive. Cops can't protect you.'

Hot sour bile bubbled up my throat. 'How did that

happen? I mean, I've got a teenager to care for. And a new house.'

Wal kept patting my shoulder. 'Either you take control, call the shots, or roll over and be dead. What's it going to be, love?'

Wal had never called me 'love' before. It bought tears to my eyes. Last night had been endless and I didn't feel at all equipped for a new day. But wallowing had never been my way. Joanna had seen to that.

I straightened my back and rallied a smile. 'I'm going to have a shower. I expect Pete will be here any minute. Can you let him in?'

Wal nodded his approval. He looked older today, his face greasy and lined with fatigue. But his eyes were sharp and I drew strength and comfort from the grey aura that circled mine. Whatever happened, Wal would be there for me. It would be all right.

Chapter 22

I emerged, scalded, and tender from the shower ten minutes later, scraped my hair back tight, threw on a black t-shirt and jeans and went downstairs.

Cass was up and cooking oats in the microwave for Pete and Wal. She saw me and went straight to the fridge to get out some juice.

Pete paused mid-spoonful of yoghurt, looking guilty that he was partaking. He had a plaster across his nose, and two black bruises under his eyes.

Jeez. Maybe I had broken it. I held out my hand. 'Phone?'

'Nope. Just a message.'

I inclined my head to suggest we should adjourn to the front office.

He followed me out there with his yoghurt.

'Well?' I said.

He shoved his hand in his pocket and pulled out a receipt from Macca's. On the back was written, Caltex

North Freo. 'Sarge says, just go into the ladies and wait 'til it's empty. Then knock on the back wall.'

'You're kidding me,' I said.

He shrugged and began ripping the receipt into tiny pieces. When he was done, he scrunched the pieces into a ball and jammed them in his jeans pocket. I watched the procedure intently.

'What time?' I asked.

'Now,' he said. 'Bin a long night.'

'You were there?'

He hesitated, wondering what he should and shouldn't tell me.

'You're eating my yoghurt, Pete,' I reminded him.

'I was lookout,' he said. 'Few blocks away, watching out for the Five O.'

'You've been watching too much American TV,' I said. 'Are you coming?'

'Nah. Been told to stay here.'

I narrowed my eyes. 'Tell the others I'll be back in a little while.'

I let myself out quickly through the front door before Wal could find me and insist on coming. He'd done enough to protect me in the last few hours. I had to manage this meeting on my own.

The morning traffic was starting to build as everyone headed to their day jobs. I felt a moment of regret that I wasn't one of them. It would be nice to dress in a skirt and shirt, put on pumps and do the office thing for a day. Or to be catching a plane somewhere for a meeting. I imagined packing my suitcase and telling Wal to keep an eye on Cass. I pictured calling Joanna from the Qantas lounge and complaining about the lack of multigrain bread.

I ... stopped myself. Life was real; not daydreams.

Shit was real.

My phone rang as if a solid reminder of that fact. I answered and hit the speaker. 'Tara Sharp.'

'It's Lloyd Honey, Ms Sharp.'

'Lloyd? Is everything alright.'

'It is. I managed to find some information for you. I hope it's not too late to be useful.'

'I thought that you—'

'We've worked around the problems we've been encountering.'

'Oh. OK well. Can you email it to me? I'm just going into a meeting.'

'Certainly. As we speak. Have a fine day, Ms Sharp. Stay away from the streets of Cottesloe. I believe there's been trouble in paradise.'

'Shocking,' I said.

'Shocking,' he agreed. 'Take care.'

A few minutes later, I pulled into the Caltex. Before leaving the car, I checked my email. A quick scan of Lloyd's message confirmed that Freddie the Frog had familial connections with Johnny Viaspa, and that he'd had two short stints in prison. Once for theft and once for blackmail. There'd also been a case of aggravated assault but the victim had dropped the charges and without their testimony the state hadn't been able to bring a case to court.

Nice guy.

Freddie had been working at the Leederville Hotel as bar manager for six months. Before that he'd waited bar at Cable Beach Resort in Broome, until he'd been sacked for repeatedly being late for work.

And then it struck me. I knew who'd killed Bernard Romeo. And the realisation was crushing.

But I had to deal with this meeting first and I thumped my fist to my chest to shift the paralysis that had settled on it.

Cars queued at the bowsers of the Caltex station. I pulled in and parked in the bays, expecting a crowd, but the rest room was empty. I went straight over to the back wall and knocked.

A few seconds later, the back wall-panel creaked and opened inwards. A hand grabbed my wrist and hauled me through and I found myself in a small, dark room at the back of the service station. Jake Stranger was seated on the only stool. Bon Ames pulled me into the room and shoved the wall back into place.

'Very secret service,' I said.

Neither of them spoke. Their auras were murky and ill-defined in the darkened room.

I stood, sweating under their silent scrutiny. 'So?'

'Where is it?' said Ames in his most intimidating voice.

I didn't see any point in playing dumb. 'Somewhere safe.'

Ames produced a pistol in a holster and a screw-on, barrel-shaped metal piece, which I imagined was a silencer, from a kit bag on the floor. He set it all down on the filing cabinet next to him. 'What'd you tell the police?'

'Nothing that involved the Cheaters.' I stared at him steadily, refusing to be cowed by the weapon, despite my stomach hurting from the rush of adrenalin.

'What did it involve?' asked Jake, speaking for the first time.

'My client's wellbeing.' I crossed my arms.

Bon Ames and Jake exchanged glances.

'Now I have a proposition for you,' I said. 'I know what the list is for. I know what it's worth to you and … other parties. I'll make sure you get the only copy, in exchange for you giving me and my people protection from those who will be … disappointed.'

Bon Ames let out a rumble of objection and his hand moved towards the pistol.

But Jake Stranger grunted at him, and Bon withdrew his hand.

'What kind of protection?' he asked.

'I don't know,' I said. 'Just let relevant parties know that we're off limits, or they'll have trouble with you.'

'Why would I do that?'

'Because I'll tell the police every damn thing I know about the Cheaters, including the connections you have internationally.'

'You're optimistic that you'd make it out of this room to do that,' he said coolly.

'I don't have to make it out. The information is ready to go to the police if I don't return.' I'd used this tactic once before. With Viaspa. Call it blackmail, perhaps, but I liked to think of it as meeting fire with fire.

Jake stared at me for a long time before he replied. I could hear my heart, Bon's heavy breathing, smell our combined sweat.

Finally, Jake stood up and came closer to me, so Bon Ames had to step back.

'You've got balls,' he said. 'I think that's why you might live to go on that date with me.'

'Ovaries actually,' I replied.

He laughed. Once. Short. Like a gunshot in an empty street.

I drove out of the Caltex station and took the next left turn to get onto the beach road. When I got to South Cott,

I called Phoebe.

'Tara? What's happening? The police have been here twice. They said you'd told them you were working for me.'

'I'm down at the foot of your street. Parked looking over the beach. We should talk.'

'I have work I have to attend to.'

'It will have to wait,' I said firmly. 'I'll expect you in ten minutes.'

'Very well. If you insist,' she said, clearly not liking my tone.

'I do,' I said and hung up.

While I waited, I got out of the car and sat on the pine railing around the car bays. The sea was a royal blue, sparkling with morning sunshine and smelling profound and pure. I inhaled deeply a few times, hoping that it would centre me and give me strength. My life had taken some unexpected turns that I had to deal with whether I wanted to or not.

Phoebe arrived on foot dressed in tailored capris and an expensive blouse. She wore sunglasses and a straw hat against the glare. Everything about her was fresh and wholesome, but I knew that was a lie. Her aura was roiling a little quickly around her, as if it was running to keep up with her life. I knew how it felt.

'What is it? I can't stay too long. I have to be out at a brunch in forty minutes,' she said.

'You didn't drive?'

'I thought this would be easier.'

'I know you killed Bernard,' I said bluntly.

She froze. A statue of elegance ruffled only by the breeze catching in her shirt sleeves, and lifting the brim of her hat. When she didn't react, I went on.

'I'm tired, and not feeling very patient, Phoebe, so don't pretend. As my client, I wanted to give you the opportunity to handle this your way. Go to the police, get your father's people to help you, get a lawyer. Whatever you need to do. Otherwise, I will go to the cops with what I know, and you can be hauled in publicly. The press is already all over the street shoot out. They'll be sniffing around for anything that washes up.'

'And what do you think you know,' she said stiffly.

'I believe that you found out that Bernard was a drug dealer, and wanted to break it off. But he wouldn't. You knew what it would mean for you and your family if it came out, so you had him tied up and drowned.'

'That's preposterous,' she said. 'Have you lost your mind? You think I consort with ... killers?'

'I think you met Freddy the Frog when you were at Cable Beach Resort last New Year's Eve. He probably bought drugs from Bernard. And you saw an opportunity to get rid of your problem.'

'You're mad.'

'No. I'm sure if the police check into it, they'll find that

Freddy was working the bar at Cable Beach when you were there. If they ask around, check video footage, they'll no doubt come up with the proof that you two had a conversation at some stage. Which will prove that Freddy didn't just start harassing you after Bernard died. I'm thinking that part of your deal with him was that you'd hand over the list in return for the murder. Freddy, no doubt, wanted to impress his cousin Johnny Viaspa, by taking control of the gym drug trade. You only brought me in to the picture to distract everyone from the truth. Make you look as though you were a victim. And potentially find a way to have a hold over Freddy.'

When I finished speaking, Phoebe's face twisted into a cold fury. 'I wasss a victim,' she hissed. 'Bernard was a predator. He lied, and he used me. And then he wouldn't let me go.'

I nodded with sympathy. 'I know what it means to be trapped, Phoebe. But you crossed a line that can't be uncrossed. I'll give you twenty-four hours to go to the police, or I will.'

She shook her head vehemently. 'You do that and I'll bring you down with me.'

I was too numb to be bothered by her threat. It was hollow and she knew it. 'Twenty-four hours, Phoebe. That's all.'

Then I nodded to her in the way that old school acquaintances do, got in Mona and drove home.

Wal was pacing the front office, waiting for me when I got home. I let myself in quietly and forestalled his scolding by whispering, 'The deal is done. Where's Pete?'

Wal jerked his head toward the kitchen.

'I need to copy the USB,' I said.

Wordlessly, he handed it over, and I took it upstairs where I made two hard copies of my own. I hid the copies in my room and the original in the air vent in the corridor at the top of the stairs. Then went down to the kitchen.

Cass and Pete were cooking a meat sauce together. She was chopping something green to go in it and he was stirring. It would have been sweet if the circumstances had been different.

I handed him the USB. He tucked it in the top pocket of his leather jacket.

'I havta go,' he said to Cass. He pulled the pot off the burner and gave us all a vaguely regretful look.

Cass was the only one who returned the sentiment.

When Wal returned from letting him out, I sagged against the kitchen bench.

'I'm going to catch some sleep,' I said. 'Don't wake me for anything less than Armageddon.'

Chapter 23

I woke around lunch time, still exhausted, to the smell of Bolognese sauce. My stomach led me back down to the kitchen where Wal and Cass were eating bowls of sauce and spaghetti and peering at a magazine together.

'What's that?' I asked, yawning and collecting a plate from the drawer.

Wal put his food down on the bench and muttered something about having to go check he'd locked up his flat. Cass took my empty plate and began serving me some pasta, ignoring my question. I'd probably have let it slide being only half awake, but the photo at the top of the article caught my eye. Nick Tozzi was easy to pick. I rubbed my eyes and picked up the mag. It was the glossy 'Weekend' insert from today's newspaper.

I'd always loathed social pages in things: giving value to occurrences that were not in any way inherently valuable, to me at least. But this ... photo of Nick, Toni Tozzi and me together in an awkward moment at the

Hilton fashion parade. This was like having pins stuck in my eyes. The fringe of my skirt was all askew revealing a wrinkle of cellulite along the top of my thigh. Tozzi's expression was *guilty as charged*, and Toni was shaking her finger at us both.

Jeez didn't cut it. 'For fuckssakes!' I blurted out. The caption read:

Caught in the act for charity.

Cass shoved the plate of spaghetti under my nose, forcing me to take it and snatched the magazine away. 'Stupid magazine,' she said. 'I was just going to throw it out.'

Without warning, I burst into tears.

Cass tossed the magazine into the sink and threw her arms around me. We stood together—me clutching the plate, Cass clutching me—like that until my sobbing exhausted itself. When I was done, she went and dug a clean tea towel out of an unpacked box to wipe my face.

'I'm supposed to be the one doing that,' I said. 'You're supposed to be the blubbing teenager.'

She smiled. 'You do pretty good most of the time.'

I smiled back. 'I hope Eireen Tozzi doesn't see it. I'll get another call to visit.'

We both giggled.

Then I straightened up and looked around, suddenly realising that the kitchen bench was laden with dips, sliced vegetables, and I spied a plate of prunes wrapped in bacon next to the toaster.

'Devils on horseback?' I said. 'What's going on?'

'Surprise,' she said. 'We're having a housewarming.'

'When?'

There was a knock at the door.

Her smile got wider. 'Now. Can you answer it; I gotta get the mini quiches out of the oven.'

'Mini quiches?'

'Frozen ones,' she said. 'From Wal.'

Slightly stunned I walked over to the front door and peered through the crack between the frosted glass and the door jam. It was Wal. And Liv.

I flung the door open and embraced my Aunt with enthusiasm. She laughed and kissed me back.

'Show me in, silly girl,' she said. 'I haven't got rid of my hospital legs yet.'

Wal and I guided her over to the couch and they sat down together, holding hands.

'Drinks coming!' yelled Cass from the kitchen.

'They most certainly are,' said a voice from the open door. It was Bok, waving a bottle of champagne at us. Smitts and Henry followed him in.

'Henny?' I said, feeling my eyes widen.

He shook his finger at me. Then gave a bright and forgiving smile.

We were all right.

I cheered, and went to out to find enough glasses for the fizz.

Cass's face was flushed from the hot stove and with little girl excitement as she loaded mini sausage rolls onto a tray alongside the mini quiches.

'This your idea?' I asked.

'You can be mad at me later,' she said and took the tray through.

I trailed after her with a stack of cups and glasses and set them down on the crates Cass had cleared to use as coffee tables.

Hoshi and JoBob walked in together as I handed Liv a re-purposed vegemite jar. Hoshi and my parents had met before, and suddenly the room was a buzz of cross-conversations, and awash with champagne and pastry crumbs.

Then a loud knock on the still-open door preceded Ed entering the room juggling a bottle of red wine, a Beats Pill, and a pot plant. Bok took the pot plant from him and set it down next to Buddha. Cass pounced on the music and switched it on.

The affecting tones of Lana Del Rey sprang from the speakers and seemed to expand everyone's largesse. They settled in, laughing and drinking and eating while the songstress crooned in the background. Their auras glowed and mingled in a swirling rainbow of colours.

I watched them with swelling emotion in my heart. I'd made a second deal with the devil today, and I had no idea what the future would bring for me. But I did know, that right now, with these people here, everything was …

perfect. Except for one thing. Nick.

On cue, my phone rang. I stepped back into the kitchen to answer it.

'Tara?'

'Nick?'

'I'm sorry.' He sounded edgy, unsettled.

'For?'

'For pushing you. Taking you out in public when you weren't ready. When we weren't ready.'

'You've seen the photo in the magazine,' I said.

'Yes. You were right about it. It was unfair of me. And I wanted you to know something.' He sounded a little breathless. 'You still there?'

'Yes.'

'I've decided to take a few months holiday in Europe, sort my head out. Work out how to properly disengage from Toni. So, it's properly over.'

'Oh,' I said, my heart sinking. 'Good idea, I suppose.'

'I'm glad you think so, because I'm at the airport now. Boarding any minute. But I wanted to tell you how much I care about you. How much you lift me up. How amazing you are. And I had to know the answer to a question before I went …'

'What's that, Nick?'

'*Please* Tara, will you wait for me?'

About the Author

Marianne Delacourt is the pseudonym of a successful Australian sci-fi fantasy author who is sold throughout the world. Sharp Shooter and Sharp Turn are set in Perth, where the author grew up. Too Sharp, book three in the Tara Sharp series, is set in Brisbane where Marianne now lives.

Sharp Shooter

Tara Sharp Book One

Marianne Delacourt

Availiable in paperback and ebook

Tara Sharp should be just another unemployable, twenty-something, ex-private schoolgirl ... but she has the gift—or curse as she sees it—of reading people's auras. The trouble is, auras sometimes tell you things about people they don't want you to know.

When a family friend recommends Mr Hara's Paralanguage School, Tara decides to give it a whirl - and graduates with flying colours. So when Mr Hara picks up passes on a job for a hot-shot lawyer she jumps at the chance despite some of his less-than-salubrious clients.

Tara should know better than to get involved when she learns the job involves mob boss Johnny Vogue. But she's broke and the magic words 'retainer' and 'bonus' have been mentioned. Soon Tara finds herself sucked into an underworld 'situation' that has her running for her life.

Winner of the Davitt Award for Best Crime Novel and nominated for a Ned Kelly Award for Best First Crime novel. Killer Nashville Silver Falchion Finalist

Sharp Turn

Tara Sharp Book Two

Marianne Delacourt

Availiable in paperback and ebook

Tara's quirky PI business is attracting some even quirkier customers. She's not sure how Madame Vine's Escort Agency got her number. And then there's the eccentric motorcycle racing team owner, Bolo Ignatius. Both these clients want to Tara to investigate suspicious circumstances that turn up dead bodies. That can only mean one thing in this town: John Viaspa. Tara goes in for round two with the local crime boss, while balancing the tight rope of her deliciously complicated love life.

Tara Sharp's life can only be describe as furious fun.

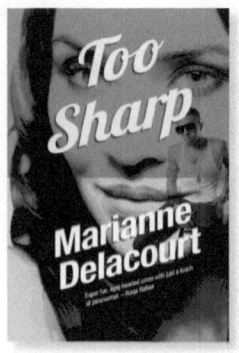

Tara Sharp Book Three

Marianne Delacourt

Availiable in paperback and ebook

Tara Sharp's new case brings her to Brisbane, where she is placed in charge of Slim Sledge, a high-maintenance rock star. Tara's a sucker for a backstage pass, and it'll provide some much-needed distance between herself and her mother's not-so-subtle hints about getting a 'real' job, not to mention crime lord Johnny Viaspa, the only man on the planet who wants her dead.

She expected the music industry to be cut-throat, but Tara soon uncovers more problems than just Slim Sledge's demands and his rabid fans. Everywhere she turns, the grudges run deeper and the danger ramps up.

Has Tara finally pushed her luck too far?

Book 1 in *The Café La Femme* series

Livia Day

Availiable in paperback and ebook

Tabitha Darling has always had a dab hand for pastry and a knack for getting into trouble. Which was fine when she was a tearaway teen, but not so useful now she's trying to run a hipster urban cafe, invent the perfect trendy dessert, and stop feeding the many (oh so unfashionable) policemen in her life.

When a dead muso is found in the flat upstairs, Tabitha does her best (honestly) not to interfere with the investigation, despite the cute Scottish blogger who keeps angling for her help. Her superpower is gossip, not solving murder mysteries, and those are totally not the same thing, right?

But as that strange death turns into a string of random crimes across the city of Hobart, Tabitha can't shake the unsettling feeling that maybe, for once, it really is ALL ABOUT HER.

And maybe she's figured out the deadly truth a trifle late…

Shortlisted for Best Debut Book, Davitt Award for Australian Women's Crime Writing

Killer Nashville Silver Falchion Finalist

www.ingramcontent.com/pod-product-compliance
Lightning Source LLC
Chambersburg PA
CBHW020539020726
47494CB00006B/1837